what passes for love

a collection of short stories

stan rogal

INSOMNIAC PRESS

Designed & edited by Mike O'Connor
Copy edited by Lloyd Davis & Liz Thorpe

Canadian Cataloguing in Publication Data

Rogal, Stan, 1950–
        What passes for love

ISBN 1-895837-34-0

I. Johnson, Kirsten.   II. Title.

PS8585.0391W53 1996   C813'.54   C95-933019-4
PR9199.3.R548W53e 1996

Printed and bound in Canada

Insomniac Press
378 Delaware Ave.
Toronto, Ontario, Canada, M6H 2T8

acknowledgements

Several of the short stories contained in this book have been published previously: *Skin Deep* in Glimmer Train; *Freckles* in Quarry Magazine, *Late-Night Subway* in Fiddlehead; *Home, After All* in Blood & Aphorisms; *Exhibition* in Playing in the Asphalt Garden; *We're Right in the Middle of It* in Dandelion Magazine; *The Ant Game* in The White Wall Review; *A Taste of Apricots* in Playing in the Asphalt Garden.

paintings by Kirsten Johnson

to robyn – stories and stories

skin deep

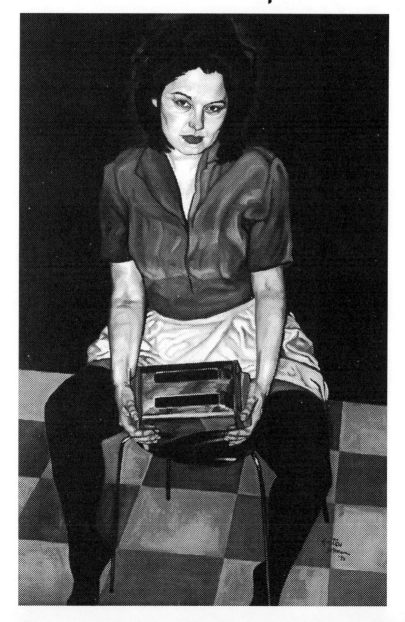

I t started a few months back. My wife waking up one morning with someone else's leg. The left leg, I remember. If she was aware of the fact, she never said "boo" to me about it (which was typical for her, her being the type who needed to *work-things-out-for-themselves*, leaving everyone else in the lurch), and, of course, I never mentioned a word to her. How could I? I mean, it's not as though she couldn't know. How could she *not* know? Waking with one new leg; one leg entirely different from the other? Well, not that they were *that* different, you understand, but different enough. Different enough to *know*, that's for sure. I mean, it was plain to me from a quick glance and she was the one — what? — *wearing* the damn thing. It may have been embarrassing for her. I wouldn't doubt it. Which may be the reason why she didn't bring up the subject. I'll tell you, she was very quick to cover herself with the blankets when she saw me staring at her legs. Her *leg*. Should I have said something then and there? Confronted her? No. Best not to speak about it. Not yet, at any rate. Leave it in her ballpark. Let her choose the time and place. I could wait. Meanwhile, I watched to see how she would adjust (or how she *could* adjust, I mean, who could guess what sort of life this leg was used to?) It didn't take her long, actually. I was quite amazed. Oh, she was a bit rocky at first; stumbled getting out of the bed, wavered slightly as she stood, stubbed her toe (the big toe on her *original* leg, which makes some sense, I suppose, since it was the one suffering at a disadvantage, it attempting to behave *as expected* and being shanghaied at every turn) against the foot of the night table, staggered toward the bathroom and very nearly crashed into the door frame. Still, once she exited the shower she appeared to be more or less in control and, for the few days that followed, I was hard-pressed to notice any discomfort or difficulty at all. In one way I was pleased with her ability to adapt (she was not one who readily forgave awkwardness of any sort, in herself or others). Conversely, the better she handled the situation, the less likely (or willing) she'd be to confide in me. Which seemed to place me in a rather peculiar position, as if I too sported this foreign leg and was similarly required to realign my parts, my actions, in order to accommodate it. This felt unfair. Still, rather than cause any sort of disagreement or ill-feeling between us, I let things remain as they were, even to the point of not questioning her present habit of changing in the bathroom or wearing long nighties to bed. She was obviously distressed and I knew her well enough not to provoke her with even the mildest sorts of interrogation. Better to let sleeping dogs lie, though I'm unsure as to how much sleep the situation allowed either of us. Certainly, I had problems logging even a couple of hours each night, so imagine her stuck with x pounds of flesh and bone with a mind of its own. Anyway, no sooner had I become almost content with this conclusion when I discovered that her other leg had been replaced. Or transformed, I don't know which. She'd kicked the covers off in her sleep (her semi-sleep) and the hem of her nightie rode just below her hips. Her legs were perfectly illuminated, bathed in a slice of moonlight. There could be absolutely no mistaking and I thought, perhaps now, she'll speak. Such was not the case. If anything, she became more silent; more reclusive. I began to fear that there was more to this than met the eye, though I couldn't think what. I tried dropping hints; asked her how she was feeling, whether her back was giving her problems, did she want her *legs* massaged? With each remark she became more irritated until I thought she'd fly into a rage. I decided it was best for all concerned to drop the matter. If she could live with two new legs, then so could I. If only it had ended there, I think I could have been accepting. It was her arm next. Her left arm. Then in rapid succession her right arm, her left shoulder, her right shoulder, her left breast, her right breast — my wife was transforming before my very eyes, metamorphosing into...who? Someone else. A wholly new person. And also, *unknown*. Completely unknown. It was frightening to watch her, as well as painful. Indeed, it was even problematic. I had to secrete myself in corners, peek through keyholes, drill tiny holes in walls, carefully peel back the many layers of clothing she wore to bed and study her under the thin glow of a pocket flashlight. I admit, for a time I began to wonder if it was me rather than her who was undergoing a transformation. I mean, none of our friends said anything (but then, why should they, being friends?) When we *saw* our friends, that is, which we don't, anymore, for one reason or another. A decision was made (or not) by one of us or both of us (I *think*, I can't remember) and we stopped. Strangers, on the other hand, would stare and mutter to each other, the way strangers do, at least implying that *something* was noticeable; something was odd. But *what*? My mind filled with doubts. Like, I *knew*, in my heart of hearts, that my wife formerly had a mole on her right shoulder and that *now*, it was gone. And yet I wondered, was there ever *really* a mole there, or was her shoulder always so smooth, so white? Were her breasts (which I once knew intimately and which now I find grotesque, unable to touch them, barely able to look at them except as cold, objective evidence) actually larger or smaller than these she now carries? I took to memorizing what was left of her (what I *knew*, or thought I knew, to be left of her). I made notes. I drew rough sketches. The changes continued: her back, her tummy, her buttocks, her hips, that gently matted area she once described as containing "the jewels of the mountain." I compared the new parts with my notes and sketches. They were similar, yes, but not the same. Definitely *not* the same. Hadn't the navel once been round and now it is oval? But then, what is the difference between the words "round" and "oval" and how much does it take, really, for one to become the other and vice versa? Hadn't there been more hair lodged between her legs? Or were the sketches poorly drawn in the first place due to the dim light? Had I smudged whole areas in my haste? I mean, I'm no artist, and yet...This morning her face had transformed. How could I ever forget or mistake this? Its shape; the precise position of her eyes, her nose, her lips which I had kissed thousands of times in the past? The manner in which her hair curled and fell. It did curl, didn't it? Yes! It did curl! In lovely blonde (brunette? auburn?) tresses draping across her shoulders (or short-cropped, straight above her ear lobes?) But what does all this matter, these "physical" things which are highly problematic at the best of times and really next-to-nothing in themselves anyway? It is her behaviour which is most indicative, most revealing; her actions; her attitudes. These are what show her to be *other-than-herself* and so, *suspect* (if not thoroughly dangerous). She has become distant, secretive, even hostile. I recall one or two times when she had discovered me jammed into a closet or pressed against a window or waking some nights to catch me "examining" (her word) her like some "insect" (again, her word) under a microscope and "What the hell was I doing? What was I looking for? What was wrong with me?" With me? She still refused to admit, still refused to take me into her confidence, and so I'd have to make up some excuse like, I lost my pencil (and what was I writing, a letter to my dead mother?) or a match or I was merely interested in the pattern on the sheet. Lame, I know, but better than forcing the issue (and who knows [and why not?], perhaps she had become accustomed, was even *happy*, with what was happening to her). At any rate, it is reasonably clear to me that I am losing my wife; that, inevitably, either tomorrow morning or the morning after or the morning after that (one morning, for sure), I'll wake beside a woman whose entire inner workings will have metamorphosed; whose mind will have shifted to such a degree that her memories will consist of a different life, a different house and, more-over, a different husband. In short, this woman will wake to see me as a perfect stranger in her bed. Then, what calamity will occur (for a calamity *must* occur, make no mistake)? She might scream. She might run into the street calling for a policeman. She might attempt to run me through with some sharp object. Naturally, I've taken certain precautions. I've hidden her scissors, her knitting needles, her nail file, her shoes with the spiked heels. I've removed any blunt, heavy objects. I've even taken the glass from the picture frames. I know all of this is driving her crazy; she can't find a thing she's looking for, but, better safe than sorry. I've emptied the savings account, the car is gassed up and ready to roll, my bags are packed, there's a Smith & Wesson under the pillow (though I'm not so sure it hasn't changed by now as well, having shed its metal skin and lies in wait, coiled and fanged with the oily aspect of a rattlesnake). Well, whatever. One can only prepare for so much. The rest is simple accident.

freckles

W ell, like they say: *the worst I ever had was great* and, yeah, to be honest, this time it'd been OK. It wasn't bad. It was all right. I mean, what can you expect? It's a natural progression, right? You sleep with the same person over and over and it can't always be like in the movies, all bells and fireworks. That goes without saying and you have to accept it as fact. And not only her — me too. Me too. You know, sometimes you're not quite into it, or you're tired or there's something weighing on your mind — whatever — yet somehow you want to a little bit more than you don't want to (this is you or the other person or the both of you now, you understand) or you figure it might be just what you need at the time when maybe it isn't or — who knows? And so you do. You do, and usually, for the most part, it's OK. It's nice. You do it and no one's nose is out of joint and you say goodnight in a civilized way and you roll over and go to sleep. And that's how it had begun.

We had climbed into bed and she said she'd like a little snuggle, and there had been no hint beforehand and it was the furthest thing from my mind, but I thought, sure, what the hell, why not, and I obliged, except during the whole time after she'd got me up and in, she sort of disappeared on me, you know? Like her mind was fixed on something other than the fact of me working away inside her. Which, again, was not unusual. I mean, I knew by this that she was not in the mood for an orgasm, just a snuggle, and I could enjoy myself and not have to worry about her. So I did, then rolled off and gave her a hug, a kiss; you know. It was OK, like I said. Nice. It was nothing new up until then, only this is the time she decides to tell me, while I'm lying back all comfy-cozy, relaxed and loving her, right? I mean, on the one hand, you'd think that would be the absolute worst time, but on the other, it makes a lot of sense, when you think about it. I mean, the same sort of thing happened when she banged up the car. And when she quit her job. She waited for the exact same time to tell me. And you can't blame her. I mean, there is no best time or right way. What I'm saying, I guess, is that it's something like when the cat drops a dead bird at the foot of the bed — you're sorry for the bird, but the cat's just trying to make up for something or show its affection and it's not really the cat's fault. Of course, this was something entirely different and really not in the same category at all as cars and jobs. I mean, you know what I'm talking about. This was different. This was something else and I don't have to spell it out, you understand. I mean, to tell the truth, I have a lot of trouble even thinking about it, never mind saying it. For her though, the words just spilled out. And maybe that's best too, in these situations. No fancy footwork. No beating around the bush. Just sharp and clean, like the surgeon's knife, *zip*: "I've been sleeping with someone else." Just like that, she says it, and it's out in the open, hanging in the air like some kind of...I don't know...thing. I can't describe it. I can't begin to describe it.

You're kind of stunned at first, and then all the machinery starts in motion and it's all automatic and you've got no say in what happens after that. And this is really funny (not funny, y'know, like it wasn't funny; no one was laughing; I sure as hell wasn't laughing; it was strange is what it was; strange-funny) because the first thing that popped into my head wasn't the first thing that I would've expected, given the circumstances. And maybe that's the way it happens all the time too, for everyone, I don't know. Maybe there's been a study, but I haven't heard of it. It's sort of embarrassing now, I guess, to say it, but the first thing that popped into my head — and remember, I had absolutely no control over this myself — the first thing was: Betty; which makes me question what the hell goes on inside a person, eh? Really. I mean, you think you've got a pretty good idea about who someone is, or a better idea about a close friend or the person you're married to, though not completely, not everything about them. So you count on a few surprises now and then, but with yourself, you figure you should know what to expect in a given situation. Right? Well, no way. I never expected this. Not in a million years. But there it was.

I started thinking about Betty and that time two years ago. I couldn't help it; I could only lie back and watch. It was her last day with the company. As the story went, she had a job lined up in Vancouver and she was hopping a plane early the next day. So the girls had prepared a little do for her in the afternoon — wine and cheese and stuff — and the guys could drop in or not. There was nothing too personal between Betty and me, we were on speaking terms and that was about it. We worked in different areas of the company, our paths crossed occasionally, we said *hello-how-are-you*; that sort of thing. Still, I stopped by and offered my best wishes. To tell the truth, I was more interested in the drinks and sandwiches. Not that there was anything wrong with Betty. She was nice enough. A bit on the quiet side; shy maybe. She wasn't my type, that's for sure. Not bad looking, but twenty pounds overweight and red hair, which never appealed to me. And *freckles*, man, did she have freckles. Her face and arms were covered with them. I don't know, I could never see myself going to bed with a woman whose breasts were freckled. Or her pussy. Don't ask why; it's just something that puts me off.

At any rate, she split early (she said she had to do a few last-minute things and finish packing) and I hung around making small talk with the rest of the girls until the wine was gone.

I was going to go home after that, but decided I wasn't in the mood. The wine had given me a bit of a buzz and I felt like continuing. Besides, the wife was out for the night taking a drawing lesson, then dinner with a friend, etcetera. Perfect. I jumped into the car and drove to a bar I knew closer to home. There were plenty of places nearby, but I like to avoid being flagged over by the cops if I can help it. Also, the job situation's tough enough as it is without being spotted by a client or a boss or even a fellow employee. The word gets around, the story grows, and the next thing you know, you're pegged as someone with a problem. After that, it's a short walk to the unemployment line.

Anyway, I arrive at the bar and who do I see but Betty, sitting at a table in the corner, by herself and working on what turns out to be her third rum and coke. Now, I never in my wildest dreams would've expected to see her in a place like this, alone, drinking double rum and cokes, but there she was. Well, if she hadn't turned at that moment and spotted me, I probably would've just backed out and left. I didn't want to be involved. But she did see me, so I walked over and said hello and she started crying. She had been crying but now she really broke down.

Seems she wasn't going to Vancouver after all. Her boyfriend had dumped her, she was pregnant, she had planned to go in for an abortion, except now she wasn't sure if she wanted to go through with it; like, maybe she should have the baby. You could've knocked me over. Who'd've thought it?

I tried to console her; bought her another drink, wiped her eyes, *yeah, most men are assholes* and so on and so forth, and...to make a long story short (don't ask me how it happened, it just did) we ended up going at it in the back of her van (now that's another thing...I never much saw her as a *van* person either, but there you go) except, when it came to the crucial moment, that is, when she'd made up her mind to write the boyfriend off for good and she was ready for me to slip it in, I suddenly started thinking: *What am I doing? I'm happily married. I've been married for eight years and I haven't screwed around once. Maybe toyed with the idea once or twice, that's natural, but never done it. I love my wife. I love my kids. Do I want to maybe lose it all for this? I mean, who is this woman? What is she capable of? She's in a desperate position, after all.*

So, I tuck it back in my pants. I tell her she's a bit mixed up at the moment, a bit drunk (I'm a bit drunk) and I don't want to take advantage of her and everything will work out in the end, etcetera. And I zipped up and left.

I never saw her again. I don't what happened to her. She might've thrown herself in the lake for all I knew. I felt bad. I did. But what else could I do? I checked for her name in the papers for weeks. I watched for her at the bar. Nothing. No sign. So, I more or less forgot about her.

And then, the next thing, I'm lying there in bed and my wife is telling me what she told me and I'm thinking: *What a first-class jerk. Why didn't I do it when I had the chance? I could've. I should've. I was a fool not to.* I mean, what a stupid, middle-class, bullshit attitude, you know? What I'm saying is, that's what I mean when I ask what goes on inside someone. I mean, what was it that made me think that way with Betty two years ago and what was it that made me think of her after my wife told me...you know, and I was lying there? I don't know. All I know is, that's what flashed through my mind. I couldn't think of anything else, only: *You dumb bastard!*

So I got up, cleaned myself off, got dressed and walked out the door. I didn't say a word. I must've had some idea of where I was going, what I was going to do, but I'm not sure. Mostly, it was a blur. It was like I'd shifted into automatic pilot. I was totally out of touch. I certainly wasn't inside myself. No way. I was further outside myself than I think I'd ever been. It was like watching a movie of myself. One of those old home movies, all grainy and jerky.

So, what did I do? Just what you'd expect. I drove to the liquor store. Except it was closed. It had been closed for hours. I thought: *For chrissakes, what sort of anal retentive country is this that prevents someone from buying a bottle after 9 p.m.?*

Then I remembered there were a couple of bottles of red wine under the seat. I'd bought them for something. I don't know what, but sure enough, there they were! Now that's more like it, I thought. I cracked one and started guzzling. I just kept driving and drinking until the bottle was empty.

Next thing I know, I'm pulling into the parking lot of a bar — the *same* bar, mind you, which I guess is no big deal since I'd often come by since, it's just that things seemed to be adding up to something in a peculiar way. I tossed the empty into the back and tucked the full one under the front seat.

I went into the bar and ordered a scotch with a beer chaser. I knew the guy behind the bar. His name was Dave. He asked how I was doing and I told him terrific, never better. He said that's the way and gave me my drinks. I didn't want to talk. I wanted to be drunk. That's it. So drunk that I wouldn't have to face all those questions I knew were bound to arise surrounding that single statement: *I've been sleeping with someone else.* But it's like when someone you love dies. You can all of a sudden consume vast quantities of alcohol to no effect. Or maybe you are affected but you don't know it. Maybe you have to rely on a second opinion to know what shape you're really in. I asked Dave.

"Do I look drunk to you?"

"Man," he said, "from where I stand, if you can ask that question you must be either very drunk or very sober."

So there you go. I finished the scotch and ordered another. I began to look around the room. There was a guy playing piano. Not very well. A regular. I'd seen him before. There were two couples shooting pool. Another couple sat holding hands at a table. Around the bar there was an old Chinese gentleman dressed in a black suit and a white shirt. He looked like an undertaker. He was reading a racing form and sipping on a beer. Two seats away from him was a woman, forty-fivish, skinny with too much make-up, grinning beside a young guy who was entertaining her by rolling a coin between his fingers. She'd take long drags from her cigarette, tilt her head back and blow smoke in a line toward the ceiling, where it would quietly explode.

Then I noticed, way back in a corner, in a booth, sitting alone, a red-haired woman, and I thought: *no, it can't be, not after two years, not tonight.* Yet she looked familiar. I asked Dave what she was drinking and he told me double rum and cokes. He smiled. I ordered another scotch, another beer, a rum and coke and headed over.

It was Betty all right, and she recognized me. She offered me a seat, pleasant-like, as though we had just seen each other yesterday. She looked good. Thinner, I thought. We talked. Not about anything. Just talked. We ordered more drinks. I crept closer to her, or she crept closer to me. At any rate, we were soon pressed together in the booth, whispering to each other, rubbing our hands over each other's legs beneath the table. When the bar closed, Betty said she was in the mood for another drink. I told her I had a bottle of wine in my car and asked her if she still owned that van. She did. I grabbed the jug and away we went.

I thought, this time things will be different. Nothing unexpected. Last time, we were piss-eyed drunk; our clothes were half-on, half-off. I remember wanting it that way: I didn't want to see her body. I thought it might disgust me, so I'd kept my eyes closed, or else fixed on an earring or a small white area on her cheek. This time, I wanted to look. I wanted to see her pale skin swarming with reddish freckles. I undressed her slowly, undid her bra and placed my finger on a freckle that sat on her chest at the point where the breast begins to swell. Then I placed my finger on another, and another. I began to count them, even though I knew it was impossible. My finger travelled slowly down and around her nipple; then to her belly, her hip, her thigh and between her legs. Her body rose toward me; she grabbed hold of me, pulled me on top of her and guided me inside her. I felt her freckles shift between our flesh like strange, exotic fish. At least, I imagined it was happening. It was beautiful.

When we were done, she left. There was no mention of the past, no messy questions about what we do next or where do we go from here. It had happened and it was over. I got into my car and went home. What else could I do?

I pulled into the drive, parked, got out, walked up the steps, through the door, into the living room and down the hall. I pushed open the bedroom door. There was my wife, still sitting up in bed. And there, also, was me, my head tucked beneath her breasts, against her belly. We were both crying. She was rocking me in her arms, saying: *Don't cry. Don't cry.* My finger was tracing a tiny freckle on her hip. My lips were moving. I was counting.

late-night, subway

H e is the only passenger in the car. Not too unusual. He works until midnight, always has a few beers to unwind, catches the last subway train home. Once in a while he goes the whole trip without seeing a single person get on or off. Once in a while. Though not often. More often there are others. People like him who work late, or party late, or are night-owl/insomniac types, or have nowhere else to go, nothing to do. Who knows; maybe there have always been folks getting on and off and he failed to notice. Maybe. Though he suspects not. He maintains a peculiar pride in considering himself quite perceptive in this matter. It's a game with him: people-watching. Try and guess who they are, what they do, where they're coming from and going to. Depending on his mood and the amount of beer he's consumed, his imaginings fluctuate considerably and a shabbily dressed individual might take on the attitude of a disguised prince, while a prince (though admittedly a rare bird on the public transit system, there have been well-documented sightings) may prove to be a down-at-the-heels actor out performing for quarters. Particular times he will tap the shoulder of some such person and ask their business, just to see how close he came to the truth. But no...he never does and for obvious reasons. Obvious to himself. Such as: TRUTH IS A BORE, or, I CAN'T BE BOTHERED, or, I DON'T WANT TO GET IN THEIR WAY. In hard fact (in cold truth), he is merely frightened. Not of anything specific; anything you can put your finger on. His fear is irrational. Moreover, he knows it, which only makes things worse. A friend once said to him, if you're so scared, get a gun. Like telling a drowning person to calm down with a drink of water. Face it, if someone like him is walking around carrying a gun, what are the rest sporting? Like, a soldier got on the train one time. He *seemed* to be a soldier. Dressed in army fatigues and toting a gunny sack. There was an ID tag strung through a loop on the sack and the writing on the tag was foreign — sort of pictorial. Where did he come from? Anything could have been in that sack. A bomb. A machine gun. A capsule of poisonous gas. It makes you wonder: why would a soldier want to kill the passengers on a subway train at two in the morning? The answer is: why not? There are things at work in the world — forces — that we simply cannot comprehend. There are plans in the machinery that will not show themselves for generations. Who knows what effects might spring from apparently minute and meaningless actions? These are processes that are felt rather than known. When the soldier disembarked there was a clearly audible sigh of relief from the car. Whoever the poor bastards were who were targeted, it was not those present on the train.

He is the only passenger in the car. Not too unusual. He considers the fact that the train makes every stop. The doors open, the doors close, no one gets on or off. A waste of time and energy. He's on his way home. It's costing him time. Except, he isn't in a hurry. He experiences no sense of loss. So long as he's home in time to turn around and go back to work, he doesn't care. The train is comfortable. He's never bored. He can read the advertisements. TAKE THE BUS TO MON-TREAL! He doesn't mind the bus part, but why would he want to go to Montreal? GIVE THE UNITED WAY! You bet. Comes right off the old paycheque and the company matches penny for penny. THE CARAMILK SECRET! Cute. Tiny elves drilling holes into the chocolate. Things they do to grab your attention. Still, he thinks, how do they get the caramel filling in? A gorgeous babe kisses a guy's cheek because of the cologne he wears. Definitely. Believe it. AFFORD-ABLE DOWNTOWN CONDOS STARTING AS LOW AS $199,000! He doesn't think so. BLUE JAYS' BASEBALL! CALL FOR A BLUE! Right on! Should've had another one tonight. Enough time, just...Just what? DO YOU KNOW SOMEONE WHO'S AN ALCOHOLIC? Man, he thinks, if he's an alcoholic, everyone's an alcoholic. Couple of beers. He counts the empty seats: ninety-six.

He is the only passenger in the car. Not too unusual. Though unusual for this long. Normally fun to try and guess how many people will be at the next stop and what they'll look like. The beautiful blonde that catches your eye and it's instant meltdown. Oh yeah, baby! Except, the expectation tonight is zilch. Or else a phoney blonde packing a chainsaw, or a pack of wild dogs, or a bunch of zombies with blood dripping from their teeth. He should be so lucky. Meaning, when a figure appears on the platform, he is not overly enthusiastic. No bodacious blonde, no crazed mutts or recycled corpses. A woman. A woman reading a magazine. Well, the ground shifts but the game stays the same. Will the car stop in front of her? Will she enter? It does; she does. He picks at a thread in his pants and peeks at her. There are six empty seats immediately around him. She will move deliberately to a seat on the other side of the train to him and back. This is natural behaviour. It shows confidence and provides an air of casual indifference to the situation. To behave any other way would be to show: 1) that she has noticed him, and 2) that his presence governs her choice of seat. In other words, to move too slowly, with too much forethought, is to show fear. He decides on the seat she will most likely take. His eyes lean further toward the thread. Her eyes remain glued to the pages of the magazine. She sits beside him. What? He freezes. Something is not right with this picture. Not because she isn't the beautiful blonde and their eyes failed to meet in a way that promised the gates of heaven etcetera. No. That is fantasy plain and simple and not something he gives in to, only explores; like going to a movie you know will end in two hours with you leaving the theatre on your own, though a bit more warm and glowy. This is a different animal altogether. His body shrinks to allow as much distance between him and her as possible. She, however, is expansive, her entire form breathing the limit of its space and encroaching barely on his, with the threat that, at any moment, their peripheries may come into contact and the two will touch, be it ever so lightly. His knees clench as if in slow motion, obtaining the tightest character while rousing the least suspicion. What is she thinking, to sit so near to a perfect stranger, alone on the subway, at this hour of the morning? Is she a hooker searching for a last trick? If so, she has a funny way of making a john feel comfortable. He doubts it. He knows the behaviour of hookers. She'd sit directly across from him, playing with the hem of her skirt, smoothing her legs, fondling her breasts, getting his attention with a lick of the lips, a roll of the eyes. She is no hooker. Not even dressed like a hooker. Plain. A few pounds overweight. Wrapped in a dull beige trenchcoat. Her feet hushed in sneakers. Little make-up. How can he tell? He sees her reflection in the window across the aisle. Definitely not his type, yet…alone on the train, a few beers, 2 a.m…. Has she even noticed him? Not likely. So engrossed in her magazine she doesn't realize. And if she does (*when* she does), what then? An embarrassing position for them both, he guesses. Perhaps if he knew what she is reading? Impossible to read the title of the magazine in the window. He could turn his head to the magazine itself, but that would be too obvious. He knows one must be delicate. He straightens and leans back, keeping his hands in his lap. In his lap? He quickly clasps his hands and manoeuvres them to the left side of his hips, careful not to touch her accidentally with his right elbow. Now his head is behind hers. Good. There she is in the window. If she glances up, she'll see him sitting beside her, gazing at her in the window. But, she doesn't glance up. She reads, with a sort of intense relaxation.

How nice that must be, he thinks, to be so absorbed in a single activity; to be so calm and assured, without any visible thought or effort. Is it the material in the magazine? Or the mere act of reading? He braves a brief glimpse — almost a non-glimpse. *Something* LIFE magazine. She's reading a magazine called *something* LIFE. He feigns a yawn and manages a closer look. An advertisement for a new car. How can anyone be so intent over an ad? AUTOMATIC TRANSMISSION, standard. ANTI-LOCK BRAKE SYSTEM, standard. ALL-WEATHER RADIALS, standard. COMBINATION AM/FM RADIO/CD PLAYER, standard. Well, that's a nice touch. THE ONLY THING THAT ISN'T STANDARD IS THE PRICE. Maybe, but can she afford it at any price? Does she really want to buy a car or does she just like the ad? Is she fantasizing? Does she have a general interest in cars? Perhaps she's an auto mechanic? Or is she actually aware of the situation she's gotten herself into and is covering herself within the glossy print of this ad? If he keeps his head behind hers then turns and leans toward her he can put the reflection of his tongue into the reflection of her ear. He's played this game in the past. Often. No harm done. He doesn't do it now, though; he doesn't quite trust her. He grins a little grin remembering all the ears his tongue has tickled. When the correct moment presented itself. Unbeknownst and all. CHRIST! She moved. She shifted her weight in the seat. Her left knee tipped outward. He could feel it tap his right knee. He *can* feel it. What to do? To move now would admit their knees are in contact; would admit his discomfort. Why hadn't he removed his knee immediately? Because his thoughts were elsewhere. Because he had allowed his mind to wander. Not *allowed*, exactly. It just *had* and now he was having to pay the price. Of course, the longer he failed to act the more difficult it would be. But then, why should he be the one to restore equilibrium? He had done everything in his power to preserve a safe and reasonable distance between the two of them. She's the one constantly overstepping the boundaries. She's the one who should furnish a remedy. Unless she desires physical contact? Is that it? Is she making a play? Perhaps she's lonely. Perhaps she's one of those married, middle-aged women who roam the streets for some anonymous excitement. Is she wearing a wedding ring? Difficult to tell. The reflection shows numerous rings. Is one a wedding ring? Remember, the reflection reverses and distorts, so that...But, wouldn't she remove her wedding ring if she was on the prowl? Not necessarily. He squints in an effort to further consider her reflection. She ain't ugly, he thinks. Ain't beautiful, ain't ugly. Just kind of...hard to judge really, with the magazine blocking the lower half of her face. Handsome eyebrows. Not too thick. And her nose is...classic! The way it sits like that, between her eyes. Cheeks a tad on the chubby side. She might be a bit younger than she looks. Or older. Not bad, overall. Hold on a second, he thinks. Let's not get carried away. The whole thing might be an accident. Best to suss out the situation. Make sure. I'll just cough, he decides, move my knee and see if she goes for me again. He coughs. Nothing happens. Their knees remain flush. Did he move or only think he moved? Did she follow his move? He coughs again. His leg twitches. Their knees stay together. OK, he thinks, two can play this game. He reverses the tactic, applying pressure to her knee this time. That's odd. There appears to be no resistance.

Not no-resistance, where we say a woman resists the advances of a man, just, her knee provides no physical resistance to his own. His knee, in fact, seems to sink into her knee, as in quicksand. He, naturally, cannot see this, only *feels* it and is, understandably afraid to investigate. Instead, he squeezes his eyelids shut, concentrates on his leg muscles and, beginning gently, then actually straining, tries to ease/yank his knee from hers. Nothing. Nowhere. Struggle as he might, he is unable to produce any motion in an opposite direction. He relaxes, opens his eyes, stares into the window and down to the seat. As he suspected! His knee half-hidden in hers. Yet, this is impossible, and he knows it. His knee, he thinks, is not being eaten by hers. This is a trick of optics aided by her soft flesh, her loose clothing. But why is he unable to separate his knee from hers? Likely the leg has gone to sleep. He *believes* he is in control of his muscles when, in truth, the muscles are numb. What he must do is shift his entire weight a few inches to the left and drag the dead portion with him. She can interpret his action any way she wishes. Absorbed as she is in that magazine, she'll hardly notice or care one way or another. Besides, what would she imagine anyway, to witness his knee practically on top of her own? No, this is by far the best course of action, though requiring a certain amount of delicacy. He manages a space between the two of them by wiggling his butt back and forth and sliding to the left. He unclasps his hands, stretches his back, slips his fist into the crack and prepares to raise himself for the final push. She adjusts her position. Not largely and with simple ease. The back of his wrist brushes her hip. He images the wrist and hip coupling like two train cars. She continues reading. What can he do? Tell her they

are joined at two locations? No. The story is too pre-
posterous. She'd think he was crazy. Show her? Again,
no. Who can tell what her reaction might be? She
might get violent and perform some damage upon him
or to herself. Either way, given the situation, he'd suf-
fer. He is familiar with stories of Siamese twins. The
fact that one can get drunk and leave the other to suf-
fer the hangover. Or have sex and leave the virgin sister
pregnant. And when one or the other died, the second
follows rapidly. Is this his fate? To be welded to this
woman for life? They'd have to find work in a circus.
But what circus would have them? They'd be suspected
as frauds. Siamese twins are always the same sex.
Who'd believe a man and woman without some idea of
underhandedness? Besides, we're different colours.
Many things can be explained away to chance or cir-
cumstance, but not biology. The train jars and his
hand and elbow melt into her. Moreover, his knee has
all but vanished along with a portion of his thigh. Is
now the time to panic? The woman remains focused on
her magazine; unconcerned; unbothered. A cool head,
he thinks, is the requirement. Stay calm. If this is happening (and there is the possibility that it isn't), then
he must be prepared to weigh alternatives and cope
with new developments. Still there is no denying some
sense of urgency. He is in up to his shoulder, down to
his ankle. He twists his body as best he can and reaches
down with the pretence of retrieving an object from
the floor. He clutches his pant cuff and tugs. No use.
The foot stays wedded to hers. He yanks at the cuff. It
tears and the entire foot snaps out of sight behind an
old white sneaker and a red sock. She's wearing jeans
under her coat, he notices. His leg and hip fight
against the undertow and are lost. Everything is occur-

ring rapidly. He raises his left foot and jams it between the seats, uncaring whether she spots his strange behaviour or not. If his actions irritate her, she'll have to deal with them in her own way as best she can. He is losing his shoulder. Impulsively (to save his own neck, so to speak), he aims to brace himself against her body with his left leg. The leg fails to secure solid ground and dissolves before his terrified eyes, sucking his hip and back in along with it. He cranes his neck and cranks his head in an effort to keep from drowning completely in this impassive sea. He focuses on the side of the woman's face. How radiant she appears, bathed in the sharp contours and merciless white light of the train car. So round. So soft. So beautiful. Everything goes black. He opens his mouth as if to speak, then, perhaps thinking better of it, perhaps not knowing what to say, closes his lips and feels his skin enveloped in warm, moist darkness. The train stops. The doors gape. The woman lowers her magazine, rises from her seat and exits, walking briskly along the platform toward the stairway. The doors shut. The train is swallowed by the tunnel.

home, after all

— for Raymond Carver

W hat is it?" There is no reply from Jim as he continues working the key into the lock. "Is something wrong?" Still no reply. Harriet adjusts the weight of her shoulder bag. "Is it the right key?"

"Course it's the right key."

"Well…"

"It's not the key. The key's working." Jim leans into the door and gives it a slight push.

"Stuck?"

"No. It must be the deadbolt."

"That's not possible."

"Maybe not. But I think it's on."

"Then Bill must be inside. Or Arlene."

"Why would they have the deadbolt on?"

"How should I know? Habit, maybe. Maybe they're…busy."

"Busy?"

"I don't know." Harriet stares at Jim for a second, then shrugs. "So, knock!"

"What, on our own door?"

"Why not?" Harriet prepares a fist, but before she can get into position, the door opens a crack. A length of chain secures the gap.

"Who are you? What do you want?" A man's face peeks from behind the door.

"Bill?" asks Harriet.

"Bill! What's going on? Let us in."

"I don't know you. Go away. Go away before I call the cops."

"Bill…" The door slaps shut.

"Bill? Bill! What's the matter with you? We're home."

Jim is about to hit the door when he's stopped by a second voice.

"My husband means it! Go away or we'll call the police."

"Arlene? It's us! We're back." Harriet raps on the door.

"I'm going to count to three. If you're not gone by then…Honey, pick up the phone. One…two…"

Jim and Harriet take a step back and whisper to each other.

"So, what do we do?"

"I don't know. What can we do?"

"Well, one thing's sure, we can't do anything out here."

"Right."

"We could go into their place and phone them?"

"What, you think they didn't recognize us or something?"

"Maybe. I don't know."

"OK. Fine."

Harriet takes a key from her purse and unlocks the door across the hall. They enter the apartment. Jim walks over to the phone. He puts down his suitcase, picks up the phone and dials.

"Uh-huh. Right."

"What?" asks Harriet.

"Busy." Jim tries again, then hangs up. Harriet drops her shoulder bag to the floor. She places her suitcase on the dining table, opens the case and removes a small bag. Jim watches her. "What are you doing?"

"I want a shower."

"Here?"

"They won't let us in our place, and I want a shower. I'm sweaty from the flight."

"OK. Just don't be long. We have to discuss this." Jim heads to the kitchen. "I'm going to pour a drink."

"Bill only drinks bourbon."

"So?"

"So, you don't like bourbon."

"Uh-huh?" He takes the bottle from a cupboard. "Y'know, the sonofabitch was wearing my housecoat."

"You sure?"

"Sure I'm sure. You want one?"

"Might as well."

She goes up the hallway to the bathroom. Jim pours two drinks. He knocks one back in a gulp, then pours another. He knocks this one back as well and pours again. He carries the glasses to the fridge and sets them on top. He grabs a couple of ice cubes from the freezer and drops them into the glasses. He bends to look into the fridge. There's some leftover chicken on a plate. He pulls off a leg and begins chewing. Between bites, he sips at the bourbon. He unwraps a few ham slices, rolls them around some sweet pickles and eats them. He finishes off the last slice of an apple pie.

"No point going hungry. Goddamn crazy bastard," he mumbles.

He licks his fingers and closes the fridge. He pours more bourbon and reaches in his pocket for a cigarette. The pack is empty. He tosses it on the counter and moves back to the living room. On a side table is a tobacco pouch and half a dozen pipes leaning in a holder. He fills one of the pipes and lights up. He takes off his jacket, loosens his tie and removes his shoes. There's a pair of slippers next to the couch. He puts the slippers on his feet. He stretches out on the couch; smokes; drinks; stares at the slippers. The phone rings and he answers it.

"Yes? Who? No, this isn't…I mean, yes, yes it is. I am. Who's this? Oh. Well, no, I don't think…Really? Really. Well, that does sound like a damn fine offer. Sure. Put me down. The whole apartment. Furniture too. Why not? This Thursday will be fine. Yes. See you then." Jim grins, then laughs.

"Harriet? Harriet?" He listens for the sound of running water. Instead, he hears a door close. "You won't believe what I just did." He downs both drinks, goes to the kitchen and pours two more. He adds the last of the ice cubes then refills the trays and places them back in the freezer. He steps out of the kitchen as if expecting Harriet to be there.

"Harriet? Honey?" He wanders down the hallway and sticks his head into the bathroom. There's no one there. He enters the bedroom and sees Harriet sitting at the dresser, primping before the mirror.

"What are you doing?"

"You mean this?" She rises from the stool and models a black lace bra and panty set. "I found it in the closet. Isn't it absolutely wicked?"

"Yes. But, do you think you should? I mean…"

"Why not? Fair's fair, after all." She looks at Jim's feet.

"New slippers?"

"They were just sitting there. On the floor. I slipped them on."

"Is one of those for me?"

"Hm? Oh, yes. Yeah." He hands her a glass. She sips the bourbon and grins.

"Smell here." She wraps her hand behind his head and draws him to her shoulder. He sniffs. "Now here." She moves his head to her neck. He sniffs. "And here." His head is lowered between her breasts. He sniffs. "You like? It's new."

"Very nice."

"Mm. You too. You smell…sweet."

"It's the pipe tobacco."

"Mm. I like it." She kisses his hair; the top of his head. "Now, are you going to take me to bed, or what?"

"Here?"

"Of course, *here*. Why not *here*?"

"Maybe I should try calling again?"

"What's the hurry? Relax. Have some fun. They're obviously not going anywhere tonight."

"I guess you're right. Nothing we can do. Plenty of time to straighten things out later."

"Sure. Why not take advantage?" She climbs into the bed.

"Oh…did you want me for something earlier?"

"Huh?" Jim fumbles with his belt.

"Earlier. I thought I heard you calling me."

"Earlier? Oh, yeah. I remember. One of us has to be home Thursday morning."

"Thursday?"

"Yeah. Someone's coming by to clean the apartment. There's a special." The belt refuses to release.

"Uh-huh."

"Even the carpets." He gives up on the belt; grips his glass.

"That's good. They can use cleaning."

"Yeah. That's what I thought." He suddenly turns and moves toward the hall. "I feel like another drink. How 'bout you?"

"Sure." She toys with the bra strap, then calls out. "Oh, honey? Don't forget to bolt the door."

"Don't worry. I was just gonna do that."

"Mm." She crawls under the covers, gives the pillow a pat.

"Good," she whispers. "It's good to be home."

exhibition

Karl stepped back from the canvas and shrugged. *That's it*, he thought. *Done.* He wiped his hands with a rag, lit a cigarette, inhaled, blew a few smoke rings. He squinted at the painting, picked up a brush and made a motion or two with his wrist as if he were going to make some slight alteration. Then he changed his mind. *Fuck it*, he thought, and simply signed his name to the corner.

This was the last of twelve paintings in a series, one named for each month of the year, chronicling the change of scene outside Karl's window. It had seemed like a good idea at first. Now, he was sick of the whole thing; he'd had enough. *Just wrap the bastard, get it down to the shop and stick it with the rest.*

Tonight he was to have his first one-man exhibition in a reputable gallery with a reputable dealer. The dealer had seen samples of Karl's work hanging in a local pasta joint and gave him a call offering the show,

publicity, invitations — even an opening-night cele-
bration with wine and cheese — the whole ball of wax.
Karl felt excited at the time and more than slightly
flattered. It wasn't long, however, before these feelings
were replaced by fear and doubt: fear that the work
would be unsatisfactory or that he'd be unable to meet
the deadline; doubt that his paintings would attract an
audience in any case. *Who the hell would want to come
out for me?* That was the question he posed to himself
about ten thousand times a day. *An artist? Shit, I'm no
artist. No fucking way. I never should've quit my job at
the beer store. I was making a good buck. I had a fucking
life. I must've been nuts.*

"Karl! Karl! Are you going to answer the door or
what? Karl?" Beth charged across the room in long,
determined strides. "Chrissakes, you can't even go to
the can around here."

Beth was a big woman, not fat, but tall, big-boned
and furnished with an abundance of good, solid flesh
that she carried with comfort and grace. Her dirty
blonde hair was thick and wild, managed only by Beth
constantly running her hands through it. She finished
zipping her fly just as she opened the door. It was Mr.
Mendino, the landlord. He stood gaping in the doorway.

"Well, what the hell do you want?" Beth was about
twice his size and straightened up to increase her
advantage.

"Ah, Mrs. Phillips, good day." Mr. Mendino kept
moving his eyes from Beth, to the floor, to the door
frame, to the room of the apartment behind Beth.
"Um, I wonder, is Mr. Phillips at home?" He tried to
crane his neck around Beth but she leaned with him,
blocking his view.

"No, Mr. Phillips isn't home. Why do you want him?"

"No, well, it's about the rent, Mrs. Phillips."

"Oh, now, Mr. Mendino, you know that I get paid on Fridays. That's tonight. You'll have your money tomorrow."

"I'm sorry, Mrs. Phillips, but the fifteenth was yesterday. You're already a day late."

"You'll get your money tomorrow. Like I said."

"Mrs. Phillips, please…"

"Look, will you stop calling me Mrs. Phillips. I am not Mrs. Phillips. There is no Mrs. Phillips. I am Ms. McKenzie, as you goddamn well know. Just as you goddamn well know that I get paid on Fridays."

Mr. Mendino glanced down the hall. "Please, the neighbours."

"To hell with the neighbours! Maybe now they won't have to lean against the keyhole to hear me."

"Mrs. Phillips, I must warn you…"

"Warn me? Warn me about what? The cracked ceiling? The leaky taps? The broken toilet? What are you going to warn me about? The missing floor tiles you promised to replace since the day we moved in? The fucking cockroaches? Hmm? What?" Mr. Mendino's jaw tightened. "Or maybe it's not the rent you're after." Beth took a deep breath. She was braless beneath her blouse and her breasts were large and firm. She tucked the tips of her fingers between two buttons. "Maybe you don't want Mr. Phillips at all, hmm? Maybe you're wanting to work out a little trade with me. Hmm? Is that it? Is that your game?" She undid one button. Mr. Mendino backed away, almost tripping over his own feet.

"Tomorrow," he sputtered. "I expect to see the rent money tomorrow at the latest." He turned and fled down the stairs.

Beth laughed as she slammed the door. "Hypocritical

little wop." She spun around and faced Karl. "Did you hear that shit? Him tryin' to threaten me? I had him peeing his pants."

Karl grabbed a sweater from the bedpost. "He's not a wop. He's Portuguese."

Beth shook her hands through her hair and approached Karl. "Same difference. They're both fucking sardine eaters." She wrapped her arms around his neck. "Anyway, what's the big deal? "

"You bullied him."

"I bullied *him*? That's a good one. What about the crap he tried to pull on me? And don't think he wouldn't love to get his greasy paws on me. Ha! He goes out of his way to give me the old hairy eyeball; you better believe he does."

"He's harmless."

"Yeah, like a rat." Beth leaned into Karl and kissed his lips. Karl was actually an inch or two taller than Beth, but because of his slim build and poor posture she appeared to be the larger of the two. "Oh, I know, honey. If I had invited him in you'd've just given him the money out of your pocket and everything would have been A-OK, right?" Karl didn't answer. "Isn't that what you'd've done? Hmm?" She kissed his cheek. "Honey?"

"No."

"No. Of course not, 'cause you don't have 500 bucks in your pocket, right? You don't have 500 bucks period, right? Y'see — I know that. I know that and I don't care. All I care about is you and me. Together. With a roof over our heads and food on the table and a place for you to paint. That's all that matters, isn't it honey? You and me." She slipped her tongue into Karl's mouth and directed him onto the bed. She unbuttoned her blouse. "And tomorrow Mr. Mendino will have his money and everyone will be happy again." She pulled off Karl's sweatshirt and kissed his chest. "Poor Karl. Poor, poor Karl. What would you do without me to look after you, to take care of you?" She took his hand and placed it on her breast. "Do you still love me, Karl?" She unzipped his jeans. "Do you love me?" She ran her hand beneath the elastic of his underwear. "Tell me you love me. Tell me." She kissed his neck and whispered, "Tell me."

Karl stared up at the crack in the ceiling. He knew that Beth had removed her pants; that she was naked beside him. He felt her slide down his own jeans and underwear; felt her take his erection in her hand; felt her crawl on top of him and guide it inside of her.

"I don't love you," he said. "I don't love you." He spoke into her thick hair. Beth continued to rock back and forth, oblivious to the words. Karl wondered whether he'd actually spoken the words aloud or not. Perhaps he had only thought them. Perhaps he had said nothing.

"You do love me, Karl. I know you do. I know." Beth inhaled, held it, moaned, shuddered then released her breath in short, sharp gasps. She moaned again. "You do love me." Her voice faded, "I know you do."

∂❧

Karl arrived at the gallery by cab and unloaded the picture.

"You did it then! Good for you! I wasn't sure you'd have it ready, but here it is." George Bernard was the dealer. "We could have gone with eleven, and would have, naturally, but it's so much better, I think, with the full complement, yes?" He hadn't uncovered the picture. "January through December, yes. An entire year; full circle, as it were. Ah, Karl, this is my assistant for the evening. You haven't met and you should, absolutely. Her name is Francine. She's from Montreal. Taking art history at the university. Plus marketing and sales, plus computers, plus who-knows-what-else."

"Nice to meet you," Karl said.

"You too." Francine was a reasonably attractive young woman, about twenty-five, Karl guessed; slim, dark-haired, stylish — perhaps a bit too made-up for Karl's taste, but, like he always figured, *what's my opinion got to do with anything?*

"I'm enjoying your work. You have a wonderful talent for creating mood with colour. I can't wait to see the latest piece." She took the package into the back room.

"You should get to know her; her father's a great patron of the arts. Especially the paintings by *unknowns*. Filthy rich. Into pharmaceuticals, real estate and God knows. Listen, people will be arriving shortly. Pour yourself a glass of wine. Relax. Oh, by the way, is your *friend* joining you tonight?" Bernard and Beth had met only once, but it seemed to be enough for the both of them.

"No. She's...she's working tonight."

"Ah, yes. Waitress or something, wasn't it?"

"She drives forklift in a warehouse. It's swing shift."

"Mmm. Yes. Just as well really. These things can be quite boring for the partners, what with all the attention being focused on the artist. Besides, as I recall, the two of you had differing opinions as to what a painting should be, yes?"

"Yeah, well, she kind of likes a tree to look like a tree."

"Exactly. And nothing wrong with that, God knows. Variety being the spice of life, etcetera, and no reason to cause problems for a relationship; no reason at all." Bernard headed for the back room. "Excuse me. A few last-minute details. Pour a drink and relax. I'll send Francine back out to you. Get to know each other."

"Thanks. I'll do that." Karl poured a glass of red wine and studied the paintings mounted on the wall. He shook his head. *Are these mine?* he thought. *They've got my name on them but I don't remember doing them. There's been some mistake. I don't belong here. Who am I trying to kid? I had a good job once. A damn good job. What was I thinking? I must've been nuts. I was nuts.*

ॐ

As far as Karl was concerned, the opening was a farce. No one seemed interested in either him or his paintings. People came and went in rapid succession, filling up on the wine and cheese and speaking with whomever could do them the most good. Bernard performed the polite introductions, which began and ended with the quick handshake and obligatory *well done* and *good show*. But what had he expected? He didn't know. Near the end of the evening, Francine tapped him on the shoulder.

"How's it going?"

"Fine, I suppose. No one's thrown a punch."

"This is fairly typical. You get used to it."

"Mmm."

"Really, no need to worry. Everyone knows that Bernard discovers and shows only the best of the new wave. You'll be in the morning papers."

"There were reviewers here?"

"Oh, yes. Some here, some not here. Doesn't matter. They'll all have to come up with beautiful words and grand theories to describe you and your work. Some of it may even be close to the truth. Take my advice: enjoy it, then forget about it."

"I see. It's business."

"Exactly. That's what they do. It's their job. Your job is to paint, and show up to perform the necessary social obligations. Anyway, there's a party up the street where I'm staying. Younger crowd. Not so formal."

"I don't know if I'm up to a party."

"Oh, you have no choice. You're the guest of honour. Besides, I'm supposed to take care of you; fill you in; introduce you. It's my job. Bernard tells me that you're practically a virgin to the art scene."

ॐ

Francine was right. The new gathering was less formal and the guests were younger. In fact, the suite was choked with people leaning against walls, crashing on furniture, laid out across the carpet. Everyone appeared to be smoking and the air was thick with haze. The first thing Karl did was light up, then a joint was passed his way and he took a hit. *This is better*, he thought, and started to relax. He looked around for Francine, who had gone for drinks. A woman came by holding a rolled-up bill and a small mirror with half a dozen white lines running across it. Karl passed. The woman grinned, shrugged her shoulders and moved on. Another joint made the rounds. Karl took a deep drag and held it in. It was good grass and he could feel it taking effect already.

"Hear that? That's Bird. Man, he could play."

"What?" Karl turned toward the voice. It came from a slim, pale young man with watery red eyes.

"Bird, man. Charlie Parker. You never heard of Charlie Parker?" His tone was accusatory. Karl was going to say something when another voice jumped in.

"You're fulla shit, asshole. That's not Charlie Parker. That's Dexter Gordon, man. You're fulla shit."

Karl walked away, leaving the two to argue between themselves. What did it matter to him who was playing? As far as he was concerned, you either liked the song or you didn't. Parker, Gordon — what difference did it make? It was the music that counted. Like choosing between a Picasso or a Rockwell or a finger painting your eight-year-old kid did in school — you're going to hang up the one you like and that's art. Between the wine and the dope and the bullshit, Karl was feeling testy. *Yeah*, he thought, *I'm in the mood to match my ignorance against someone else's arrogance.* At that moment, Bernard rushed over with a good-looking man in tow.

"Well done, Karl. Well done. Extraordinary. It was wonderful tonight. Marvellous. Everyone was impressed. Totally, totally — impressed." Bernard burped lightly, laughed, gave the young man a squeeze around the waist and wove his way back into the crowd.

Karl noticed that the two guys arguing about the music had called in reinforcements to back their positions. *Why not look at the name on the goddamn cover*, he thought. Then it struck him that this party was also "just business." None of these people were artists; they were the art scene. Karl looked at his hand and saw that a drink had somehow materialized. It was a large scotch, neat. He threw it back and tried to find his way to the door.

"You ready to leave?" It was Francine. "Me too. C'mon. My room is down the hall."

à

It was all too much for Karl. He let himself be led. Francine seemed pretty high herself. She was giggling and making little sighing, snorting sounds through her nose. She dragged Karl to the bed and began to undress him.

"Is this just business too?" He had wanted to hurt someone, earlier, in the other room, but it had come out now and he was surprised and angry at himself. He was about to apologize except that Francine continued without missing a beat. Had he spoken? Had she heard? She pulled down his pants, rubbed his thighs with her hands, then gazed up at him.

"It's my business." She giggled. The snorting sounds continued. She slipped out of her clothes and the two of them jumped beneath the covers. They kissed. Karl fondled Francine's breasts and her low snorts grew louder.

"Is everything all right?" asked Karl.

"What do you mean?"

"The sounds you're making…I don't know if you're excited or if something's, like…wrong."

"Oh, no. Everything's fine. It's when I drink, something happens to my adenoids; they swell or something and it affects my breathing. Especially during sex. But no, I'm OK."

"OK." Karl was not totally comfortable with the snorting but figured if Francine was really interested, he'd try and give her a good time. He licked her nipples and began working his tongue down her belly and between her legs. She stopped him and drew his head back up to hers.

"No. I know that you're trying to be sweet but, I just don't like it."

"No?"

"No. It...I just...I don't like it."

"Oh. OK."

"I should also tell you, I don't orgasm either. I mean, I do, but only when I do it myself. When I'm alone."

"Uh-huh. Listen, are you sure you want to...you know?"

"Yes. I want to. I mean, I enjoy it and all, I just don't come. So you don't have to feel obligated to, like, wait for me or anything. Enjoy yourself whenever you're ready, you know? I'll be fine."

"Fine?"

"I mean, it's all right. I enjoy a man inside me."

"You just don't come?"

"No." Francine searched with her hand between Karl's legs and found him only partially erect. "It's OK. Really."

"I know, but..." She shoved her tongue into his mouth and pulled him on top of her. Karl stiffened and was about to enter her when she snorted.

"Your condom or mine?"

"What?"

"Did you bring a condom?"

"Well, no, I didn't. I didn't think..." Francine rolled out from under Karl and produced a condom from the bedside table.

"This is the '90s, after all. Better safe than sorry. You do wear one, don't you?" She tore open the package. Karl stared numbly. "I mean, Bernard told me that you have a partner." Francine attempted to fit the rubber but Karl's slight erection withered under her touch.

"What's the matter?"

"Nothing." Karl tugged at his short beard. "I don't know. The dope, maybe. The excitement. I don't know. I have to go."

"Maybe you just need a few minutes."

"No. It's better if I go. Really." Karl slid out of the bed and got dressed. He crossed the room, opened the door and left without looking back.

❧

Karl went into the bathroom, undressed, washed, then tiptoed into the bedroom. He saw Beth curled up on her side of the bed clutching a pillow, her back to him. He slipped in beside her.

"You're late."

"Mmm."

"What time is it?"

"I don't know. Aren't you already asleep? You should be asleep."

"I wanted to know how it went."

"It went OK. I'm going to wake up famous, apparently. Like in the movies."

"Yeah?"

"Yeah." He leaned toward her. "Would you like that?" He touched her cheek and felt a tear. His hand withdrew. He laid on his back and stared at the ceiling.

"What else happened? Where were you?" Her voice grew louder. It quivered. "I want to know. I..." Her throat tightened, sealing off the words. She flipped over and placed her head on his chest. "No. I'm sorry. Don't tell me. I don't want to know. Only..." She pushed her hair back from her eyes. They were both naked under the covers. She rubbed her breasts against his arm, reached down with her hand and got him erect. She mounted him, whispering, "Do you love me, baby? Do you love me? Tell me, now. Tell me. Come on, baby." Karl remained motionless, his gaze fixed on the barely visible crack in the ceiling. He opened his mouth as if to speak, then stopped, then opened his mouth again. "Do you feel safe?" he asked.

"Safe? Is that what you asked me?"

"Yes. Do you feel safe?"

"I..." She was nearing orgasm. "Yes. It's OK. It's my period. It's OK." She rocked gently on top of him with her head buried in his neck. "Tell me, baby. Tell me you love me," she moaned softly. Karl stared at the ceiling — at the crack. His body trembled. A few tears squeezed from the corners of his eyes. His jaw and lips moved but no words were forthcoming. The crack appeared to grow bigger. *Do you feel safe?* he thought. *Do you feel safe?* Beth trembled; she breathed deeply. "Tell me, baby. Tell me. Tell me. For God's sake..."

the ant game

1. ◆ She moves along the sidewalk. How? *Briskly.* This is good. *And* she weaves. Also good. She *threads* her way through the crowd, leading with her feet, her body bending *around* and following, then erect again, almost imperceptibly. Very nice. Very, very nice. *Graceful*, in an unpractised fashion. Natural. Animal. A style that develops of its own accord from *within*, then *through* the body. She is one of the challenging types. A person with a purpose. A destination. A time constraint. This is obvious. She checks her watch and adjusts her gait. Not much. A little. The stride of her legs a *touch* longer (given the restriction caused by her skirt: tight and clinching, raised just above the knees; snug across the buttocks [a strange word, *buttocks*, no?]); her steps a *tad* quicker. No, not much, but enough to gain some distance (or *close* some distance, depending on your position). While she is likely not oblivious to her surroundings there appears to be nothing which distracts her or draws her attention for any length of time. Her head fixes straight ahead for the most part, only occasionally twisting to one side or the other. In this manner, she winds *around*, and *past*, more and more people. From a certain perspective it might almost seem that she *senses* something and is (in fact) *using* these slower bodies as blockers. *Almost*. Though probably *not*. Certainly, there are no *other* outward signs. Except for this one *thing*, she *acts* calm enough, neither looking back over her shoulder nor pushing people out of the way. She is *intent*, yes, but calm. Her walk is rapid, but not hurried. *Brisk*. Comfortable. She manoeuvres, *suddenly* (though not suddenly, merely does), between half a dozen people and, *dance-like*, without missing a beat, rounds the corner. These half a dozen *bodies* converge and advance. *Another* person (separate), steps out from a shadowed doorway brandishing a Bible and poses: "IS THERE A WAY TO SAVE THE WORLD FROM WAR, FROM CORRUPTION, FROM GREED, FROM POLLUTION, FROM EVERLASTING HELL-FIRE? YES, MY FRIEND! THERE IS A WAY AND THE WAY IS JESUS!" And the *way* is snarled; dammed by a creep of tourists, hawkers and window shoppers. If there *was* a strategy at work here, it worked. The woman has vanished.

2. This one is different. A businessman, judging from the uniform. Though maybe not. Many men wear suits and ties these days. Especially downtown. It's not unusual. In fact, it's common. Why was he chosen? I don't know. Well, *one* reason. He holds a folded newspaper in his left hand and a briefcase in his right. Again, not unusual, except, *here*, the man uses both objects as weapons. Quite unknowingly, you understand.

You've often seen the type, I'm sure. Whether male or female, young or old, fat or thin, this type manages to take up the entire sidewalk. People walking toward this type invariably give a wide berth, so much so that they invariably bump other pedestrians or scrape against walls or step off the curb and onto the street. Sometimes the results are disastrous. There are accidents. Property is damaged; people are hurt, even killed. Sometimes. The *odd* occasion. I mean, it's *on record* should anyone care to verify. At any rate, it is as if there is an invisible force field around the man, when, *in reality*, it is simply that his *body* rocks back and forth, his elbows jut out from his sides, his arms sway in all directions and *anything* in his hands (in this instance, the newspaper and briefcase) become accessories to mayhem. *And*, if it is *difficult* for anyone to avoid a *frontal* encounter with the man, it is pretty near *impossible* to go around from behind. And, *of course*, he (this *type*) is never in a hurry and is forever stopping to look into a store window or stare toward the direction of a *normal* traffic sound or at the top of a building or a gum wrapper at his feet or even his watch. *He stops to look at his watch?* Why? God knows. Naturally, this causes numerous problems behind him in terms of pedestrian congestion and pile-up, which is *annoying* in itself, BUT, what is *most* annoying is this: whatever happens as a result of his actions never affects *him* personally, nor does he accept any blame in the distress or injury befallen others. The *good* thing, I suspect (and the *reason* he was chosen), is that the man is extremely difficult to lose. Even unseen, his whereabouts are unmistakable. As now, with the crowd knotted and a few brave souls passing him via the street or fighting their way among the frantic cars in order to reach the other side. Horns blast, tires squeal, drivers rant and swear while *the man* proceeds *care-less-ly*, south on Yonge Street, then right, going west on Queen to Bay, then crossing the courtyard to City Hall, progressing through the main doors to the stairs, up one floor where he enters a large office area, locates his desk and sits. Easy. *Too* easy. One almost might have wished: a red light, a fire engine, a Bible thumper, a total solar eclipse. *Almost*. Almost, but not quite. No. *Definitely*, not quite.

3. ◆ Goes into a convenience store and buys a newspaper. OK. Buys a chocolate bar as well. OK. Comes out of the convenience store, unwraps the chocolate bar, tosses the wrapper on the floor and eats the bar. OK. Goes along the hall to the lottery booth and buys a ticket. OK. Goes out the door, down the stairs, crosses the street, enters the subway, uses a pass, goes into McDonald's and orders a burger, fries and a soft drink. The food is put into a bag. OK. Comes out, goes down the stairs, around the corner, stops to buy a PEOPLE magazine. OK. Goes down the next set of stairs and finds a place on the platform. OK. Opens the newspaper. It's the SUN. OK. Steps onto the train and sits. Reads the paper. Eats a few fries. OK. Gets out at Bathurst. OK. Goes down the platform, up the escalator, out the door, left on Bathurst to Bloor and into the bank. OK. Uses the bank machine. OK. Comes out of the bank and goes east to Brunswick. OK. Turns north on Brunswick, goes up half a block and enters the walkway of a house. OK. Goes up the stairs, puts the key in the lock, opens the door, goes inside, closes the door. OK. *Done.*

4. ◆ *"Did you hear the news? Someone was walking down the street the other day and turned into a restaurant."* (HAHAHahahaha...)

5. Her. She looks like she might be worth a *gander*. Nice legs. Nifty little outfit. Not that that matters. Still... Probably a secretary or something. Finished work for the day and going... where? For a drink? But, she wouldn't go alone. Or would she? Maybe meeting friends. A boyfriend. Yeah. Don't think she's heading home just yet. Doesn't look like it. Maybe going to do some shopping. Yep, that's it. There she goes. I'll just wait out here for a few minutes. Hope she isn't one of those *buy-out-the-whole-store* types. Nope. Out already and on the move. Going somewhere alright. Must've figured out she's running behind. I'll have to pick up the pace a bit myself if I want to keep close. Hold it! She's stopped. Howcum? I'll just duck in here. Is she looking behind her? No. She's going down the escalator. Better shift gears. What the hell! She's standing at the bottom. Waiting for me? She's not looking this way. She's opening her purse. What's she after? A can of Mace? A fucking whistle? Maybe I should just backtrack a bit. Naw! She hasn't spotted me. No way. And what if she has? I'm not doing anything wrong. I haven't bothered her. It's a free world. It's a free mall. I've got as much right to be here as she does. I can go where I want. No skin off her ass. Anyway, she's just reading something on a piece of paper. Man, now she's off and running like a goddamn rocket. I wish the hell she'd make up her mind; either go or stop... oh oh! Now what? Who's she talking to? A *security* guard? Sure as shit! And they're both lookin' this way. At me? Or someone behind me?

6. I've seen him around quite often. Usually following young women. *Usually*, though not necessarily. Young, *attractive* women. Usually. Like this one now. *Quite* attractive. Smart dresser. Terrific legs. And

nervous. He'll have trouble with this one if he isn't careful. She looks like the type who expects to bump into a mugger or a rapist every time they turn a corner. Oh — he's stopped. So has she. Does she see him? Does he *think* she's seen him? Maybe. He's ducked into a doorway. But she's on her way again and so is he. I'll just keep to the wall. Now he's stopped at the top of the escalator. No, he's on it. He doesn't seem happy though. Has he lost her? Is she down there, waiting for him? She *is* down there. She's reading something on a piece of paper. Now she's looking away. And there she goes! He's not even halfway down. He's going to lose her for sure if he doesn't move it. What's his problem? Why doesn't he go? It's like he's frozen. Oh, I see... she's grabbed a security guard. What's she telling him? That some creep is after her? Wait a minute! That's not a security guard. It's some Salvation Army guy trying to push some religious material on her. She's trying to go around him but he's not about to let her. Now they're both looking this way. At him? So what's he gonna do? He's looking up here. Does he spot me? No. He's looking *this way*, but not at me. He's checking out the whole area. What's he thinking? He looks like he's seen a ghost or something. The woman has the same look. Now the Salvation Army guy is doing the same thing — looking behind him. What the hell's going on? Now he's taking off. Where's he going? Does he think they're going to come after him? Does he think that guy's a security guard? Wait a second... the woman's disappeared! So has the Bible thumper. Now there's someone else looking over *his* shoulder. And now he's taking off! There's another one! And a woman! And that young couple! Everyone's looking behind them! Not at me. Some of them, yes. Not all of them. All over the place. Looking back behind them and taking off. They all seem scared of something. What? They're in a panic. They *see* something. They *know* something. Look at them! Going crazy! Running into each other trying to escape. Tearing at each other. Knocking each other over. Punching and kicking each other. And what about me? Shouldn't I turn around as well? Shouldn't I look over my shoulder and see if any-thing or anyone is standing behind me? Threatening me. Spying on me. Recording my every move. Yes, I should. And I do. And there is. And now I am running as well. Pushing my way through the crowd as well. Attempting to escape as well. And what about *you*? Are you now wondering too? Does your head *long* to turn? Do your eyes *ache* to see what or who is standing behind *you* at this moment? Breathing down *your* neck or pressed into a dark corner? Or have you already made the move; looked behind you? And are you now running as well?

Well, are you?

Are you?

i don't have a problem

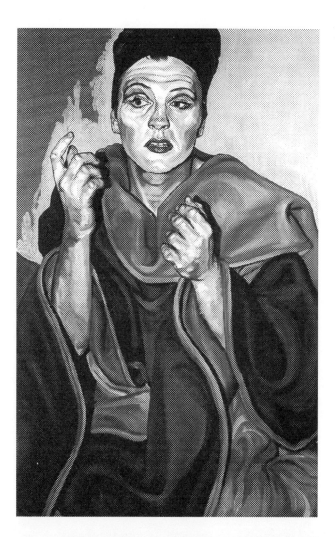

The two of them were walking up the hall, Wanda leading the way and Allan following close behind. He was humming under his breath, not a tune, not anything you could call a song or even part of a song, just a sort of nonsense; just a sort of snatch of nothing-in-particular. Wanda put the key into the lock, swung the door a crack, then must've thought better of it since she quickly pulled the door shut and turned to Allan.

"What is that song you keep humming?" Her words were short, to the point and more than a little put-off sounding.

"Song? Was I...?" Allan peered over her shoulder to a spot on the door as if trying to retrace the events leading up to Wanda's abrupt shift in gears.

"You didn't know?"

"No. I mean, I wasn't aware..."

"Great."

"It was probably nothing. Just noise. It's a habit, I think."

"Uh-huh. Listen, there's a couple of things I want to get straight right away; a couple of things you should know."

"Look, I'm sorry if my humming bothered you. I mean, it's not a *real* habit, y'know? I can stop myself. I don't have to…"

"That's not it."

"No?"

"No. That's…This is something else. Something…I want to make sure that you understand…that *we* have an understanding about a couple of things."

Allan was trying to make the leap from the 'humming' question to the 'couple-of-things' understanding, but with no luck. He shrugged and said, "OK." Not that it mattered if he said anything or not; Wanda was into her spiel and hardly took time for a breath, never mind wait for Allan to reply.

"Number one: I agreed for you to drive me home tonight because we met at Laura's party and you're a friend of Laura…"

"Yeah, well, we're…"

"Number two: I'm inviting you in for coffee or a drink because it is the least I can do…"

"I told you, it was no trouble, I…"

"Number three: I don't jump into bed with a man I've only just met at a party…"

"Hey, I never expected…"

"Number four, you saw me in that movie, *Death on the Rocks*, right?"

"Yeah, I told you. I thought you were very good." *Is that it?* he thought, *I didn't stroke her performance enough?*

"Those weren't my tits."

"Hm?"

"Those tits you saw in the movie that you thought were mine? They weren't. They were someone else's"

"Someone else's?" Allan knew that he was repeating Wanda's words. He hated when people did that to him and he hated it more when he did it to other people. It was a stall tactic. Everyone knows. But what else could he do? He was being buried, for no good reason he could figure, and no easy way out he could see. What the hell was the problem here? Wanda continued without a pause.

"Happens all the time. They hired me for my acting and they hired some other woman for her tits."

"They hired some other woman...?" He was doing it again, he knew, though it didn't seem to matter to Wanda, she had her own agenda already worked out.

"That's right. A 'body double', they call it."

"I know. I've heard of it. They made a movie...Melanie Griffith and someone..."

"Don't get me wrong. I'm not a prude. I don't have a problem being naked for a part. It's just that given a choice between showing my tits and someone else's, they chose someone else's. I didn't 'measure up.' You know what I'm saying?"

Allan didn't know what she was saying, exactly. Maybe it was the movie industry; maybe it was the fickle finger of fate. A bitterness, maybe. Thinking back over the evening he couldn't see that there had been a problem with him or with anything he'd said, though you never know. You never know what it might take to set a person off.

"Yeah, sure," he stalled, "you're saying..."

"I'm saying that I'm not the woman you think I am.

I'm not the woman you're expecting me to be."

"Look, I told you, I never…" Allan could see that, for Wanda, the pieces were falling nicely into place and she was almost at the end. If there was a picture forming, he couldn't see it; or if he could see it, it wasn't making any sense.

"The woman with the perfect tits is not me. Beneath this baggy sweater is just more baggy sweater. Now, does that disappoint you, or what?"

The pause was unexpected. Allan was still waiting for the other shoe to fall; the incriminating evidence; the piece of the puzzle that points a finger and places him at the scene of the crime. 'Does that disappoint you?' Is that what she asked?

"Well, I don't know. I…"

"You don't know?"

"What I mean is…"

"Never mind! Forget it. You don't have to say anything. It's written all over you. I should have known. As soon as you mentioned that movie I knew we were doomed."

"Give me a chance, will ya? It's not like that. I…"

"No. Forget it. It's too late. It was too late from the start. Thanks for the ride. It was nice meeting you. I'm sorry it had to end this way. Goodnight." Wanda turned the knob and entered her apartment.

"But…" said Allan, as the door closed. "Listen!" He leaned against the frame. "You're wrong. I was just a bit…surprised." He knocked softly, then slightly louder. "Hello? Hello? Can I call you?" He put his ear to the door. From inside, music played. "I'll call you." The music grew louder. Allan shook his head, turned, and made his way down the hall. Under his breath he repeated, I'll call you. I will. I'll call you.

❧

It was the following morning. Wanda was busy wolfing down a slice of toast and jam when the phone rang. She moved closer but didn't pick up the receiver. She let it ring. She let it ring until the answering machine kicked in.

"Hi. You've reached 666-6666 — ain't that the devil? Leave your name and number after the beep and I'll get back to you — when hell freezes over! Haha." There was a beep and woman's voice on the other line.

"Wanda, it's me. Answer the phone. I know you're there."

"Hi, Lees."

"Good morning. How ya' doin'?"

"Terrific. I'm on my way out."

"Where to?"

"Job."

"Which one?"

"Don't know, don't care. One of them. I'll know when I get there. What's up?"

"Can you be at an audition at two this aft?"

"Depends."

"Yes?"

"If they want me from the neck up or the knees down, I can make it."

"Don't tell me — you met another guy who saw *Death on the Rocks?* And he failed the 'boob' test; or passed it, depending on how you look at it, right? C'mon — be positive! At least you know there are people seeing the flick."

"I took the part hoping no one would see it. You said yourself it would probably never even get finished."

"I was wrong. So sue me. What have you got to complain about anyway? You've become a hot item."

"My tits have become a hot item."

"Not to worry. It's a phase people go through. Where's your sense of humour? Besides, you were blessed with a gorgeous set of breasts. Don't be so uptight; enjoy it!"

"*Breast: i) either of two protuberant milk-producing glandular organs situated on the front of the chest in the human female and some other mammals; ii) the fore or ventral part of the body between the neck and the abdomen; iii) the seat of emotion and thought.*"

"Don't tell me you have that memorized?"

"*Tit: a small or inferior horse; a nag.*"

"Wanda, you're overreacting."

"I know I'm over-reacting. I can't help it."

"It'll pass. Everything passes."

"Yeah, yeah. Like the plague."

"That's the spirit. So, can you make the audition or what?"

"If they want an actress, I'll be there. If they want a pair of tits — fax my picture."

"Wanda..."

"I'll be there, I'll be there. What's the address?"

ह

Just as Allan was about to take the step up to the restaurant Wanda came charging out the door, her coat half-on, half-off, the strap of her purse clenched between her teeth. There was no avoiding it. The two met head-on, sending Allan ass-backward to the pavement.

"Bastards!" said Wanda, then in almost the same breath, "I'm sorry. Are you OK?"

Allan got up and dusted himself off.

"Fine," he said. "No broken bones. How 'bout you? Are you OK?"

"OK?" Wanda looked at Allan as if for the first time; as if she just now recognized him. "Of course I'm OK. Don't I look OK?"

"No. No, you look...distraught."

"I look what?"

"Distraught."

"Distraught? Where did you dig that up?"

"I don't know. It was the first word that popped into my head. It seems to have worked though."

"What are you talking about?" Wanda slipped her free arm into the loose sleeve of her coat.

"You're calmer. The word, I think. It took your mind off...whatever."

"Yeah? Yeah, I guess it did. It's an odd word."

Allan wasn't sure whether he'd caught her interest or if she was only momentarily caught off-guard. The best thing, he figured, was to keep the conversation moving.

"So, what's up? What happened inside?"

Wanda was about to speak, then made the quick double-take between the restaurant and Allan.

"Were you looking for me?" The question was pointed and rather harsh. Allan could see the gears slipping into place and he wasn't sure he liked the direction she was heading.

"I wanted to see you again. Talk about what happened last night."

"How did you know where to find me?"

"Laura. I phoned you but I only got your answering machine."

"I know you phoned. How did you get my number? Laura? Christ!"

"No. I looked it up in the phone book. 'Paige' with an 'i' right? And women always just list their first initial. Besides, I knew your address."

"You're a regular Sherlock Holmes, aren't you?" She started to move away.

"That's a very interesting phone message you have."

"What do you want?" The thing about Wanda was, she didn't beat around the bush.

"I told you — I want to talk about last night."

"There's nothing to talk about."

On that score, she was more or less right. In her mind, everything was settled. The best thing to do at this point was to change the subject, put the ball back into her court.

"What happened just now? In the restaurant?"

Wanda gave a sharp glare and took a step back to the window.

"Oooooh...some 'guy,' some 'customer' thought he was being smart. Tried to play reach-for-the-glass-grab-the-breast. Dickhead!"

"What did you do?"

"What do you think? I dumped the whole tray in his lap: water, wine, fettuccine — the works. Then the manager comes running over and immediately sides with the customer without even asking my side of the story. I said, 'Listen, if I'm going to have some stranger grab my boob, it's going to cost him a helluva lot more then a ten percent tip.' She wanted me to apologize."

"Yeah?"

"Yeah. So I took off my apron and told her she could shove the job up her ying-yang."

"You seem to have this thing about your breasts."

"I don't have a *thing* about my breasts. *Men* have a thing about my breasts. I'm perfectly comfortable about my breasts."

"That's what I meant. I mean, it's not really your breasts they're after, right? It's someone else's."

"What? Oh, yeah, right."

"Can we go for coffee or something? A drink?"

"No. I can't. I've got an appointment. An audition. I've got to get my head straight." She turned and made a slight motion with her hand indicating that the conversation was over.

"What about another time?" Allan spoke to her back. "Tomorrow night?"

"Call me." Her voice trailed.

"Will you answer?"

"I don't know. I'll think about it."

ॐ

The phone rang and Wanda waited for the answering machine; waited for the voice on the other end to announce itself.

"Wanda — it's me, Leesa, your friendly neighbourhood agent. I bear good tidings." She paused for the receiver to be picked up.

"Yeah?"

"You got the part."

"You mean *they* got the *parts*."

"You want me to turn it down or what? You've got to get over this. It isn't healthy. Remember what I keep saying?"

"Yeah, I know — *Greta Scacchi*. Fine. I'll take it. I mean, it's only fatty tissue, right?"

"They said you were very good,"

"Thanks, Lees, really. Really, it's great news. It is. Maybe I can finally stop all this part-time job bullshit."

"Good girl. I'll fill you in on the details as soon as I know myself. Ciao!"

"Ciao." As she put down the receiver the phone rang again. She waited for the message. It was a man's voice. Wanda sat and lit a cigarette.

"Hi. It's me. Again. Are you there? OK. I've reached a decision. I'm going to sit here pressing the redial button and use up all your message tape until you make up your mind to talk to me. I have something to say and I want you to believe me. I'm not a breast man. Honest. Women with large, round, perfectly-shaped firm breasts don't do a thing for me. I wouldn't know what to do with them. I wouldn't know where to begin. Give me a woman with small breasts and rosy-red nipples any day. Small breasts, for me, indicate a woman of intelligence, character and bearing. It's true. Furthermore, I didn't even recognize you as the woman in the movie. If Laura hadn't told me I never would've known. Anyway, by that time I was already enjoying your company. I already knew I wanted to see you again."

Wanda gave a heavy sigh, squashed out her cigarette and picked up the phone.

"Hi."

"Hi."

"Are you telling me the truth?"

"Not entirely."

"Great!"

"I mean, the last part is true. I didn't recognize you. You look different in person. Or on screen, whatever."

"Yeah?"

"The bit about the breast size — I was trying to be funny."

"I wasn't laughing."

"Not even a little?"

"Maybe a little."

"A little is good. A little is better than not at all."

"Anything else?"

"I saw the movie again. Twice."

"Yeah? Spill any butter in your lap?"

"It was research."

"Oh — then you really are Sherlock Holmes?"

"And you know what I think? I think that's really you in the picture and those really are your breasts."

"Yeah, and?"

"So what's the big deal? I mean, it's all been done before, right? Happens all the time. You're an actor. You were doing a part. Why should it get in the way of us getting to know each other better?"

"Yeah, yeah, I know. It's just…"

"What?"

"It's new to me. And I feel…"

"Violated?"

"Christ no! Not that. It's just…the idea of meeting some guy for the first time and, even if I think I might like him, I can't help knowing that he has some sort of *intimate* knowledge about me. I guess that's it. He has an intimacy about me that I don't have about him. It's unbalanced. I'm at a disadvantage."

"Hey, if it makes you feel better, I'll show you a film of me in the buff. I'm only three, but the parts are all there."

"It's silly I know," she laughs. "I'm being stupid. So, what do you think? Still want to see me?"

"Sure. When?"

"Tonight? We could go out for a bite. Talk"

"Great. I'll be by around eight?"

"Yeah."

ॐ

Allan hesitated outside the door before he knocked, and even when he did, the knock was short and light. Wanda swung the door open with a flourish.

"Hi. I thought it was you."

"Hi." Allan stood in the doorway.

"You're right on time. I'll get my coat."

"Yeah. OK."

"Or did you want the tour first?"

"No. That's fine."

"You seem a bit funny. Anything wrong?"

"Nothing wrong, no. Just…"

"Just?"

"Well, I'm not exactly sure what it is. I mean, I think I know, but it seems ridiculous."

"So, tell me."

"I thought this would be easy. I mean, I thought that I'd have no problem."

"What are you saying?" Wanda's easy manner disappeared. "That you figured you'd just come over and I'd drag you off to bed?"

"No, that's not it. What I thought was that I'd have no problem with the breast-thing. That I wouldn't think about them; that I could just ignore them and we'd go out and have a nice evening. Get to know one another, like I said."

"Uh-huh?"

"But ever since I spoke with you this afternoon, all I've been able to think about…"

"Are my breasts."

"Yeah. Or rather, the breasts I saw in the movie. I can't get the picture of them out of my head. I mean, even when I walked through the door, my eyes went directly for...And then, talking to you — I want to look you in the face, but my eyes are drawn...down. It's crazy. I mean, you're wearing a big, baggy sweater. There's no reason, yet..."

"So what do you want to do?" There was no malice in her voice. She was more *inquisitive-sounding* than anything; almost playful. After all, there were a few directions this could lead.

"I think maybe we should pass tonight. I don't think I could take it. I'm afraid I might do something that I'll regret."

"What? Rape me?"

"No, of course not. Not *physically* at any rate. Just, 'in my head.' I don't know. It sounds weird, but there it is."

"Maybe I can put your mind at ease." She smiled and put on her coat.

"Yeah? How?"

"Those breasts you saw in the movie?"

"Yeah?"

"I told you — they're not mine." She stepped out the door.

"But..."

"C'mon, Sherlock. I'm hungry." She took him by the arm and closed the door.

"I was watching very closely."

"Smoke and mirrors, pal. Smoke and mirrors. Besides, you know there's only one way you're going to find out for sure..."

"You mean..."

"Uh-huh. But it won't be tonight."

"No?"

"No." She grinned and led Allan toward the stairs. Under her breath she hummed — not a tune, not anything you could call a song or even part of a song, just a sort of nonsense; just a snatch of nothing-in-particular.

once upon a time

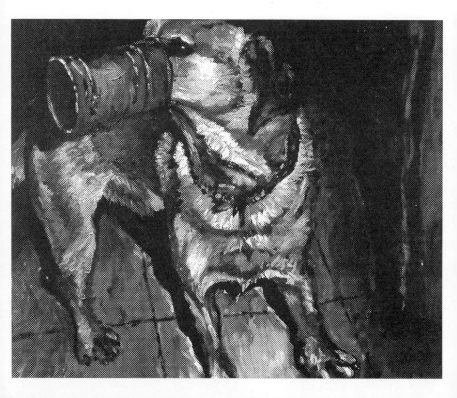

What he had told her about was a situation that had occurred a few years ago now. Quite a few years ago. Quite a few years and quite a few jobs and more than a few relationships they had gone through between them before they had met and eventually tied the knot together — more than a few *marriages*, as well, and kids scattered across the country. Norm wasn't sure how the story had even come up. It was Christmastime. They had been talking about the old days or some such thing. Nothing too serious; nothing too deep or revealing — just conversation. The story had simply emerged, as if by chance. The way Norm saw it, it could as easily have come from her. Though, maybe not. If he could have prevented himself from telling it, if he had known what effect it would have on Carol, he never would have opened his mouth. At least, he would have thought twice. Then again, one thing had seemed to lead to another and, who knows? Also, they had been drinking Glayva. That must have been it — the Glayva.

Norm was in university at the time. He was finishing a BA in English before getting his teaching degree. Along the way he was taking a couple of theatre courses and doing a bit of acting.

"I was in a play that was closing and there was an after-party in the space," he'd told Carol. "The space was the basement of an art gallery in Gastown. A woman came over to me and said hello. Her name was Amber."

"You remember her name?" Carol had asked.

"Sure. I mean, it was unusual. I've never known another Amber. Besides, I'd met her a time or two before; I'd seen her around the university. We weren't complete strangers. In fact, the last time I'd seen her was at a similar party and the two of us — somehow over the course of the evening and obviously after much to drink — managed to begin playing each other's bodies like musical instruments, keeping rhythm to the music coming from the stereo. Her date was not amused by our behaviour. It was a bit crazy, I admit, but more-or-less innocent fun. More-or-less, although, if given the opportunity…Anyway, this same guy was with her again at the after-party, but off in a corner talking with some other people. Amber said she'd enjoyed the show and I said thanks and gave a nod in the direction of her date. She was a bit high already. She shrugged and said, *he's sweet, but he's young*. I was going to ask her what that was supposed to mean when I was handed a beer by one of the other cast members.

"Another young guy joined us, an actor. He spoke rather friendly to Amber and I wondered if anything was going on between them. She was a good-looking woman and had a certain aura about her that naturally attracted men. At least, it seemed that way to me, maybe because I was also attracted. The guy wandered off after a few minutes and I said something about feeling daggers coming at me from two directions. *Three,* she said, and tilted her beer toward an older, distinguished-looking fellow who was smiling her way. I recognized him as a professor at the university. He walked over and asked if we wanted to step outside for a toke. Amber accepted. I thought it might be wiser to stay and drink my beer inside.

"When she returned I said this must be her lucky night — three men after her. I was playing it cool. She made a sound with her lips, stared straight at me and said, *only three?* She spent the rest of the night mingling with the crowd, chatting with various men, but always made a point of coming back to me. At the end, I offered her a ride home and she said OK."

"You like that?" Carol had interrupted.

"Hm?"

"Being chosen out of a field?"

"I guess. It was flattering. I mean, how often does it happen?" Norm hadn't picked up anything negative in Carol's tone. It was just a question, so he had continued. Besides, the Glayva was going down nicely and he was being caught up in his story.

"I'd packed a bottle of wine in the car in case the party moved. Amber said she had some hash at home, so away we went. Her roommate was awake when we arrived and the three of us sat around the kitchen table drinking wine and smoking hash and talking. We talked about dance, since the roommate was a dancer, and theatre, since Amber and I were into theatre, and

Edgar Allen Poe, since I had studied him and Amber was just into studying him. She told me that he wrote a particular poem — I don't remember which, *Dream Land* or *Fairy Land* or something while he was stoned. She said she knew this because she sees the same things when she's stoned. She even wrote a paper using this argument as her premise. Well, the prof wouldn't buy it — this turned out to be the same older fellow with the grass who was after her at the party — and I told her I didn't buy it either. It was too simple to call someone high or crazy rather than deal with the work. We went on like that, back and forth for awhile, then the three of us went to bed — her, me and Poe. The roommate had packed it in earlier.

"Amber had one of those futons that doubles as a couch and a bed. The place was too small for a living room."

"So she did most of her entertaining in the bed-room." Carol had spoken matter-of-factly, but to a point.

"I just meant that it was pretty typical of a student's life. Do you want me to stop? If you want me to stop I will."

"No. Go on. It's your story."

"You're sure? You're not bothered by something?"

"Should I be?"

"No."

"All right then…"

"All right. So, we pulled the futon out and made our-selves comfortable. She asked me to read her a couple of Poe poems. Partway through one of them I could see she was dropping off. Finally, she gave up trying to keep her eyes open. She gave her head a shake and told me she was sorry, but she was too tired to make it and could it wait until morning. I said sure and we rolled over and fell asleep."

"To *make it?* Is that what she said?"

"Yeah." Norm had waited for something further from Carol. When it hadn't materialized he'd topped up their glasses. It'd seemed to him that Carol was interested, or at least curious, about the outcome.

"I was awake first. There was enough morning light coming in through the window to see without flipping a switch so I poked around her bookshelf. I pulled out something by William S. Burroughs. When Amber opened her eyes she saw me with the book. '*Great,*' she said. '*I wake up with a man in my bed and he's reading Burroughs.*' I was at a part with young boys lying naked in the sun and being 'smooth and green as lizards on the rocks.'

"We drank wine and ate banana muffins in bed while she told me the story of how Burroughs and his wife were stoned out of their skulls and decided to play William Tell with a loaded gun. Mrs. B put a glass on her head while Mr. B aimed and fired. Good-bye Mrs. B. He hit her square between the eyes. Dead as a doornail.

"We made love, then had a bath together in one of those big, old bathtubs with the clawed feet. You know, the kind you can really stretch out in and relax. We went back to bed after that and had sex again. The first time we'd both been pretty drowsy. Afterward, she said we should go for a walk or get something to eat somewhere because a friend was supposed to be coming by with some coke. He wanted to get ripped, drive across the border on his motorcycle and drink some cheap American beer. She said she didn't really want to hang around and have to explain anything to him. Especially the fact that she was spending the day with me rather than him."

"And you had sex with this woman?"

"What do you mean?"

"I mean…" Carol was about to say something, but stopped herself and said instead, "Did you use protection?"

"C'mon. This was back in the Stone Age, right? It was the sixties. The west coast. Everyone was playing it wild and loose. I mean, it was her period; she was on the Pill. That's all that mattered. Nobody thought about…It wasn't an issue then." Norm had watched Carol pull away from him on the couch and he remembered thinking that the only thing to do at this point was keep on going. He had felt that it was the only way he had to make her understand; the only way he had to make her see that the story he was trying to tell her had less to do with sex and more to do with…something else. The sex needed to be mentioned, but it was bound up in something that lay outside the physical; something grander. It was nothing he could name. It was certainly nothing he could easily explain, especially in a sentence or two. It was more an idea or a feeling. The story had to do with the total being more than the sum of its parts. And one of those parts had to do with the two of them tonight — him and Carol and where they stood with each other, though Norm wasn't exactly sure how or why. He only knew that the story had to be told and it had to be told in this fashion.

"It was November. The morning was cold and clear. We walked into a little Vietnamese restaurant, pooled our money and ordered some food and two beers. There were Christmas lights flashing in the window. They must've stayed up all year. Amber said that at home, when she was a girl, her father always bought a bottle of Glayva to serve after Christmas dinner. The kids were even given a small shot. We checked the drink menu and saw that it was listed. We decided to splurge and ordered two glasses for dessert. Then we ordered two more. And two more. They were pretty reasonably priced, but we were both students, remember, and the money we had on the table was supposed to last us each the week. There was five bucks left and I said, you take it. She asked if it was enough for another round of Glayvas. I said yes, and we called for two more.

"Our conversation was Poe because I'd read him, Burroughs because I hadn't, a play she was directing, the writing we were doing or were going to do, the fact that her roommate had whispered to her the night before that she should have brought the young guy home instead of me, lousy jobs we'd had, lack of money and the complete meaninglessness of just about everything that most people find important. She told me her idea for opening a crêpe house. *Why not?* she said. *People have to eat.* She was tired of being a starving artist and tired of all the bullshit suffering that went along with it. *You only live once,* she said. Besides, she enjoyed cooking for people — she might as well get paid for it. We talked for hours and there was nothing trivial. Maybe because none of it was real. It was all dreams and dreaming. It was like a page lifted from a favourite book. It was life reflecting art and it was beautiful and it was sad and it was totally unrealistic and, I suppose, looking back, totally irresponsible."

Norm had suspected he'd used the word *irresponsible* for Carol's benefit and had given her a quick glance. She'd been sitting very still and had a serious look about her, a look that Norm was familiar with — she was turning things over in her head. Norm hadn't even wanted to try and guess. He emptied his glass and tried to wrap up his story.

"When we made our good-byes there were a few

words to do with the motion of the planets and the alignment of the stars. It was a kind of excuse because we both knew that it could never happen that way again. Not between the two of us, at any rate. We knew it shouldn't even be tried, and yet...you wonder. We didn't exchange numbers, the semester was almost over, we were headed in different directions. Everything was about to shift over a short period of time. I mean, within two years, instead of being taught, I was teaching. I was out of one world and into another. It was the end and it was the beginning and there was no escaping it. No way in the world."

Norm had watched Carol put down her glass, stand, begin to walk away, stop and speak.

"Did you tell me all this just to hurt me?"

Norm had tried to answer her, but it was impossible. He could only sit and allow her to go to the bedroom and shut the door behind her. He poured himself another Glayva. He thought about a news article he had read somewhere. It had said that more people die, get divorced, commit suicide around Christmas than at any other time of the year. It made a certain kind of sense. He tried to think back to his previous marriages in order to discover when they had finished. He tried to remember past Christmases in general. It was no use. Even last year, with Carol, was a blur. There were only small moments, flashes — and not very important ones in most instances — out of his entire lifetime that stood out in his mind. Memories. Some vague, some vivid and no way of knowing how much truth or falsehood was contained in either.

He wondered what Carol was doing in the other room; what was going through her mind. He considered going to her and telling her that what had happened was a long time ago, in a different city, under different circumstances. He wasn't the same person he was then — who is? But then he thought, what's the point? He had told the story the only way he knew how and she hadn't understood. Anything else would sound like an apology. Anyway, even he had lost the thread by now; even he had difficulty understanding both the story and why he'd brought it up in the first place. Everything was breaking into tiny bits in front of him. He was suddenly aware that nothing could be counted on. In a few days or a few weeks, tonight would be just another fading memory — imperfect, insubstantial and impossible to communicate to anyone. He'd have his version, Carol would have hers, and who knows whether there'd be any middle ground or not. Who knows whether the two of them would even be talking or even be together after tonight.

Besides, had it ever really happened to him, that evening so many years before? In that way? Had *anything* ever really happened to him? Norm closed his eyes and raised the glass to his nose. He sniffed the Glayva and tried to remember. He didn't know what. He didn't care. Anything.

we're right in
the middle of it

S o there we are, OK? I mean, we're right in the middle of it, for godsakes. I couldn't believe it. I still can't believe it. I want to pinch myself or something. He's inside me. He's moving. Everything's feeling good. I mean, everything's feeling *real* good. I have no idea. Not an inkling. I'm just enjoying it. I mean, it's the first time, y'know? The first time in, I dunno, *awhile*, weeks, that I feel like I'm going to orgasm. During the actual intercourse, I mean. Without, you know, doing something to help it along myself. I *had* orgasmed. He's sweet that way; in fact, only too happy to do whatever it takes if I'm in the mood for an orgasm. Sometimes I'm not. But when I am, he's there. You're not upset by this, right? Me telling you. The details, I mean. It's nothing new. I've told you this before, right? It's just facts. It doesn't mean anything. The point being that, during inter-course, unassisted, so to speak, it had been at least weeks; a long while. Don't ask me why it happens or doesn't happen. There's no logic that I've discovered. It's just the way I'm built; the way I am, I guess. The same as why it *seemed* to be happening then, or *going* to happen. You understand, yes? Only too well, hm? I don't know. I don't. He was the one who had started things in the first place. Which, when I think about it now, strikes me as very weird. Though, maybe not. Who knows. I mean who knows what goes on in a person's head? Anyway, we're making love, having sex — whatever — and I'm getting all warm and tingly and it's feeling just wonderful, him moving slowly in and out...I mean, I don't want to bore you with the banalities and I'm not trying to throw it in your face...I'm just telling you straight what was happening so that you'll understand, that's all. So what I'm saying is that there was nothing unusual except my feeling like I was about to come after, *etcetera, etcetera*. And maybe I wasn't paying particularly close attention or maybe I was too much into my own pleasure to notice, but, at some point, I start to feel this little quiver coming from him; from his body. And I think, oh no, not yet, not now; hold on for another minute; another three minutes. I know that sounds clichéd, but what else was I supposed to think? I mean, I genuinely needed another few minutes, simple as that. Then he quivers some more and I think this is not that kind of quiver but something else. What something else? I don't know. I start to think he's got an itch; he's got a cramp. *Don't, for chrissakes*, I think, *go and pull a muscle or something!* Not at this stage of the game. But now his whole body starts to shake. I look up at him and ask what is it? What's wrong? And his face is all contorted and I feel my mind drifting away from my body. What is it? I ask.

Do you want me to do something? What can I do? *Honey*, I say, and all feeling is leaving that part of me, right? I mean, that warm, tingly feeling is becoming like, a memory. *Honey*, I say, and he starts to heave and then he cries. First a few small tears squeezing out, then more and more until he bursts. So that's what all the quivering was about — he was holding back all these tears. Well, as if you couldn't guess, at this point any chance of anyone having an orgasm is shot to hell. His erection just goes 'blip' and he's over on his side crying and shaking and I don't know what-the-hell. *Honey*, I say. What is it? What's wrong? I want to help you. How can I help you if you won't talk to me? Well, things finally calm down a bit and he's saying he's sorry and I'm asking, sorry? Sorry for what? What's wrong? What's happened? And he tells me that I won't believe it and I say, won't believe what? And I'm waiting and I'm waiting and I ask again, won't believe what? And then he tells me, and he was right, I couldn't believe it. I still can't believe it. It's crazy.

He pulled up in a cab. He could've rented a car, but he thought it was better if he took a cab. There was less chance he'd change his mind. Or spend all his time driving around and around the block. With a cab he was dropped off at the doorstep and left there. Neighbours would see him. To walk away would look suspicious. Yes. A cab was best. He looked at the house. He didn't know what to expect. He supposed it didn't matter. The point was to go to the door, ring the bell and see what happens. He removed his finger from the button and waited. He heard footsteps approaching the door from inside. There was a peephole in the door and he expected that he was being scrutinized. The door opened. A woman stood in the opening. The two stared at each other for what could have been an eternity but which was really only an instant. The woman...the man...staring...they...

It was the damnedest thing. I had no plan. I had no idea. I just kind of rolled over and she was *there*, naturally, and I placed my hand on her butt. Her nightie had hiked up and she was warm and soft and I ran my fingers under the nightie and up and around to her breast. I started playing with her nipple and it perked up and one thing led to another and I was a bit surprised 'cause I didn't think that I was in the mood, really, and, normally, she's not a morning person. I mean, she likes to get up, brush her teeth, gargle, have a quick clean first — which never made much sense to me because she's just going to get messy and need another shower later and she doesn't like to be eaten that much, so...But, anyway, there she is getting all turned on and I'm turned on and she pulls me on top of her and I slip it in and I start moving and I'm wondering whether she wants an orgasm or whether she wants a quickie or maybe she hasn't decided yet so I keep moving nice and slow and she seems to be enjoying it, if not exactly getting into it — not moaning or anything but kind of *thoughtful*, like she might go one way or the other, but still too early to tell, so I keep at it. I'm in no hurry. It feels good. Things are going fine. I'm still not...I don't know, my brain still hasn't shifted yet; I'm still there, still making love with her, right? I'm not suddenly *off* somewhere thinking about...well, something else; something altogether different. I don't have to tell you, right? You know. I hope you know. Anyway, pretty soon I can tell she's heading toward that edge. I mean, I'm thinking that, yeah, she's reaching that point, y'know? I mean, I couldn't remember how long it'd been. Just with me inside her. No vibrator. No playing with herself. Quite awhile anyway. Quite a long time, for sure. Not that that's a *thing* with me. I mean, if she wants an orgasm, she gets one. Doesn't matter *how* you get there, right? Just get there, that's what counts. Still, it's nice every once in a while, just moving in and out and 'bingo', it happens. Like it's on its own or something. I don't know. It doesn't matter. It's happening and I'm thinking, great! That's nice. *That's nice for her.* And as soon as I think that; as soon as these words flash across my mind, I lose it. I don't know. Everything wells up inside. My guts are doing backflips. I'm trying to ignore it — what's going on inside — I'm trying to concentrate on the outside; on my dick in particular; trying to keep it up and hard and moving in and out of her. At least…at least until…But I can't. I'm a wreck. My body starts shaking and I'm crying and my…my…I mean, there's no use, it just sort of melts and I'm feeling like shit for all sorts of reasons and she wants to know what's going on and who can blame her? And what can I say? What am I supposed to tell her? So, you know what finally comes out? You know what it is I tell her? I couldn't believe it. I still can't believe it.

He pulled up in a cab. He could've rented a car, but he thought it was better if he took a cab. There was less chance he'd change his mind. Or spend all his time driving around and around the block. With a cab he was dropped off at the doorstep and left there. Neighbours would see him. To walk away would look suspicious. Yes. A cab was best. He looked at the house. He didn't know what to expect. He supposed it didn't matter. The point was to go to the door, ring the bell and see what happens. He removed his finger from the button and waited. He heard footsteps approaching the door from the inside. There was a peephole in the door and he expected that he was being scrutinized. The door opened. A woman stood in the opening. The two stared at each other for what could have been an eternity but which was really only an instant. The woman…the man…staring…they…

He tells me that he was thinking about *Sharon*. I said, Sharon? Sharon who? My wife, he says. My first wife. Your first wife? Yes, he says. Then he shuts up and just lies there again. His first wife. OK, I think, so what? A blast from the past. What's the big deal? I ask him, so…? Now get this, he says: I have to go see her. There are certain *things*, certain *matters* that have never been resolved; that have to be set straight. Well, I can't believe what I'm hearing. The first thing I think is: he's lost his mind! But then I think, no, he's serious. Something is happening; something important to him; something devastating. So, on the one hand, I'm stunned by what I feel is the ridiculousness of the situation and I want to hit him over the head and say wake up and smell the coffee; on the other hand I want to try to understand what it is he's going through. I mean, one of us has to try and be logical and calm, right? Then he says, I have to go see her. Now. *Now?* I try to talk some sense into him. Honey, I say, do you think that's such a good idea? I mean, she lives in Vancouver, we live in Toronto. And then he says something that really throws me. He says: *I think I still love her.* What? You could've knocked me over. I really did think he'd lost his mind now. But I controlled myself. I decided it was still better to try and reason

with him. Honey, sweetheart, I said, you haven't seen
or heard from her in, what? Almost twenty years. If you
went to Vancouver, what could you possibly say to
her? What could she say to you? Look at yourself. You
don't even look the same. You've gained weight.
You're practically bald. You wear glasses. You have different clothes. You have a new job; new interests. Even
your taste in music has changed. You have a different
wife. You're a different person than you were when the
two of you were together. You were just kids. She'll be
a different person as well. You probably wouldn't
recognize each other if you passed her on the street. I
mean, what do you think she'd say if you suddenly
arrived on her doorstep? I know, I know, he said. But
it's something that I've been giving a lot of thought. I
can't shake her out of my mind. I have to go. I have to.
Don't ask why. I can't tell you. I don't know myself. I
didn't know what else to say. There was nothing else I
could say. He was determined. I could see that. What
was I supposed to do? I just threw up my hands and
said, all right, if you think that's what you have to do, I
mean, if it's necessary, then I guess you have to. I guess
you have to go.

*He pulled up in a cab. He could've rented a car, but he
thought it was better if he took a cab. There was less
chance he'd change his mind. Or spend all his time driving
around and around the block. With a cab he was dropped
off at the doorstep and left there. Neighbours would see
him. To walk away would look suspicious. Yes. A cab was
best. He looked at the house. He didn't know what to
expect. He supposed it didn't matter. The point was to go
to the door, ring the bell and see what happens. He
removed his finger from the button and waited. He heard*

footsteps approaching the door from the inside. There was a peephole in the door and he expected that he was being scrutinized. The door opened. A woman stood in the opening. The two stared at each other for what could have been an eternity but which was really only an instant. The woman...the man...staring...they...

I tell her I have to go to Vancouver to see my ex-wife, Sharon. I say I think I'm still in love with her. Whaddya think of that, eh? Crazy, or what? But maybe it's better that way. I mean, she can hardly call me a liar, right? It's too weird. So, you know what she says — Go, she says. Like that. Go to Vancouver. If that's what you have to do, that's what you have to do. What do you think of that? She's a great girl, really. Totally understanding; totally unselfish. You never know until something like this comes along, eh? Not like *this* exactly, since the situation is pretty much artificial, but, you know what I mean. I mean, I couldn't tell her the truth, right? It'd be too much. It'd kill her. I know it would. She's one-of-a-kind. A real trooper. I'm just beginning to find out after all this time. 'Course, now I'm stuck having to go to Vancouver. But I'm going, all right. I have to. I've got no choice in the matter. It's all been decided. It's out of my hands. But you wanna know something really strange? The more I think about it, the more I realize that it's inevitable, the more I start to actually think about Sharon. The old days and everything. And I'm thinking, yeah, what *is* she like now? What does she look like? She was gorgeous, you know? And kind of wild. What *would* she do if I arrived on her doorstep one day? Unannounced. Offer me coffee? Kiss me? Slap me? Take me to bed? I have to tell you, I'm becoming intrigued. Does that upset you? I'm sorry if it does, but what can I say? I'm intrigued. I'm excited. It's crazy, but there it is. In fact, I've made up my mind to see her. I mean, I'm going to Vancouver. The ticket's bought and paid for. I might as well. Who knows. Who knows what might happen. Anything. Nothing. Why shouldn't I? We were married once, right? We share a past. And us? I don't know. It's all gotten so complicated. Remember the other night? You said you wished you could bring everything out in the open. I said, what do you mean, bring everything out in the open? You just sat there. That was it. That's all you said. "Bring everything out in the open." That's funny. That's a good one. As if anyone ever could.

He pulled up in a cab. He could've rented a car, but he thought it was better if he took a cab. There was less chance he'd change his mind. Or spend all his time driving around and around the block. With a cab he was dropped off at the doorstep and left there. Neighbours would see him. To walk away would look suspicious. Yes. A cab was best. He looked at the house. He didn't know what to expect. He supposed it didn't matter. The point was to go to the door, ring the bell and see what happens. He removed his finger from the button and waited. He heard footsteps approaching the door from the inside. There was a peephole in the door and he expected that he was being scrutinized. The door opened. A woman stood in the opening. The two stared at each other for what could have been an eternity but which was really only an instant. The woman...the man...staring...they...

What is it? What's wrong? Do you want me to do something? Why are you crying? Honey? Tell me.

What is it? Don't just sit there. I want to have everything out in the open between us. Honey? How can I help you if you don't tell me?

He pulled up in a cab. He could've rented a car, but he thought it was better if he took a cab. There was less chance he'd change his mind. Or spend all his time driving around and around the block. With a cab he was dropped off at the doorstep and left there. Neighbours would see him. To walk away would look suspicious. Yes. A cab was best. He looked at the house. He didn't know what to expect. He supposed it didn't matter. The point was to go to the door, walk in and see what happens. It was his house, after all, and a person has a right to make a mistake now and then. Go see his ex-wife in Vancouver? Impossible. He walked down the hallway, past the kitchen toward the bedroom. He pushed the door and stood in the opening. He looked inside. There they were. He couldn't believe his eyes. The two of them. together, naked on the bed. They stared at each other for what could have been an eternity but which was really only an instant. The woman...the man...the...staring...they...

a taste of apricots

There is a knock at the door. Perhaps a knock. Then again, it might merely be a trick of the weather. It often happens. The wind teasing the brass ram's head; the cold dragging a shudder from the bones of an ancient oak beam. Perhaps an object's dull response to some physical law — *gravity*, we call it, knowing full well that it doesn't exist. The simple attraction of a lesser body to a greater body. Perhaps a memory spun from the jukeboxed mind by a quarter so long rubbed between the fingers that both faces are blank. Perhaps a wished-for knock that repeats at precisely the same time night after night until one is drowned senseless to any real knock and whoever stands outside finally grows weary and moves on. Meanwhile, one sits alone and wonders: do they really exist, all those unknocked knocks? Or is it only at the point of contact, knuckle on wood?

He remains frozen in mid-action, like a photograph of himself, waiting for — either the telling silence or the repeated tattoo — waiting for the cue which will reanimate him, cause him to follow through with the interrupted movement (though, with a difference), or substitute a new action altogether. Years pass in this brief instant as an infinite number of stories shuffle and re-shuffle. This is not a projection. The lines in his face indicate the process clearly, even as the steam issuing from the pot on the burner acts to destroy the illusion of timelessness. Then it occurs, as surely as if it were planned — the knock. He drops the lid onto the pot and hurries to the door, his hand hesitating a moment, his body drawing a deep breath, swallowing, before turning the handle.

"Hello." A woman stands on the porch. She isn't easy to describe but she is there nonetheless. She has no traits of extreme beauty or ugliness; no limpid-pool eyes or shock of golden tresses, no distinguishing marks or scars. If she was never the school beauty queen, she was never the school hag either. Average, perhaps *too* average and it may be specifically this that makes her appear interesting: her flagrant averageness. In the background a fence, a road, a few trees, a field of corn, a low-rising hill, all turn violet in the afterglow of the setting sun. She, on the other hand, brightens in the warm electric glow of the porch light, separates herself from her surroundings and becomes more real. She is slightly underdressed for September, he thinks.

"I've been walking for miles. I must've taken the wrong turn somewhere. Would you be able to put me up for the night?" He doesn't answer.

"A piece of floor is fine. I'm comfortable anywhere." He stares vacantly at her.

"I'm afraid I don't have any money." The two face each other and, as no other words are forthcoming, he steps aside. She enters, removes her pack and coat, places them on the couch and sits. He follows her every move, never taking his gaze away. He circles her as she gathers in the surroundings. Neither speaks. The room is silent except for his carpeted steps and the creak of an odd floorboard. He stops over one loose board, looks down at his feet and shifts his weight up and down, playing the board like a musical instrument. He looks across at the woman, smiles, shrugs his shoulders. They both laugh.

Steam explodes from the pot, rattling the lid and hissing through the ribs of the burning element. No one makes a move. The woman turns toward the pot, watches the water boil over. The man pulls his lower lip with his fingers then motions halfheartedly with his head, stuck somewhere between the woman and the pot. He clears his throat and mumbles.

"That's the vegetables." She nods and he walks to the stove, one eye still on her. "I was just about to eat. Are you hungry? Would you like to join me?" He doesn't wait for an answer. Even as he speaks he sets another place at the table. "There's plenty. I've roasted a chicken. There's potatoes and carrots. I always make enough for two, that is, for leftovers. Makes things easier, you know? There's even some wine. Apricot. Homemade." He fills two glasses. "Yes? Good! Umm, why don't you come and sit here." He pulls a chair slightly away from the table. "You must be tired if you've been walking for some time. I mean, you must be tired." She sits in the chair and sips her wine.

"I'll serve." Provided with a practical task, his voice and manner liven, though with an urgency that seems out of proportion to the situation. He speaks as one who is afraid not to speak, as if only the presence of words is strong enough to hold the world together.

"White meat, I bet? Yes? I knew it. Or at least, I thought so. I had a feeling. You understand. Besides, it works out perfectly that way. I prefer dark, myself. I eat the white, of course, usually in a sandwich or something. With lots of mayonnaise. But I prefer dark. The potatoes are roasted as well…like the chicken. They're my favourite. Roasted potatoes. And there's gravy. Not out of a can. Real gravy. You like it on the meat as well, right?" He pauses, speaks lower, slower. "That is right, isn't it? You do like gravy on the meat?"

"Yes."

"Yes? Good. Gravy on the potatoes and the meat." He grins. "But *not* on the vegetables. Right?"

"That's right."

"Good! You do like carrots, don't you?"

"Carrots?"

"I could cook up a second vegetable. There's some cauliflower in the fridge."

"Carrots are fine."

"I didn't cook the cauliflower because it's white and there's so much white on the plate already."

"Carrots are splendid."

"You're sure? I have canned peas or corn. Wouldn't take a minute to heat up." He heads for the cupboard. "I realize they're not as tasty or nutritious as when they're fresh, but…"

"No, please!"

"…they're the right colour."

"Don't go to any extra trouble. Carrots are perfect."

"It's no trouble. Are you positive? I wish I had some asparagus but I'm afraid I finished it off last night." His voice stumbles, choked with the threat of tears. "I'm, I'm sorry. I wanted this dinner to be special. I'm sorry."

"There's no need. You couldn't have known. Anyway, I prefer carrots. Honestly."

"Over asparagus?"

"Absolutely. You couldn't have chosen a more appropriate vegetable. For the colour. Orange is such an indulgent colour."

"Yes?"

"Of course. Orange complements everything while requiring no complement itself. It is self-sufficient and complete, so able to give unselfishly and without end."

"Does that make it indulgent?"

"Orange indulges its own orangeness."

"A very lonely sounding colour: orange."

"Perhaps." They both laugh. She fills their glasses; he serves the food and they eat. There is no conversation. He eats slowly, his attention focused more on her and her movements than on his own food. Her eating is steady and involved, with only the occasional glance in his direction. As she eats, her food divides into separate piles of chicken, potatoes and carrots which she tends to work down evenly until she reaches the last forkful of potato. She wipes up the remaining gravy on her plate with the potato and slips it into her mouth. Before she has a chance to chew it, he calls: "Wait!" She freezes, her eyes fixed squarely on him. "There's something there," pointing at her lips. "A hair, or something." She slides her tongue out and as she does so he snatches the potato from her mouth and eats it. His eyes lower to his own plate, which is still half-full, then across to hers. She dabs her lips with her napkin. He rises slowly, takes her plate to the stove and makes up a second smaller helping. He returns to the table, smiling.

"You've got a big appetite. That's rare in a woman these days. Most women I know pick at their food. Even the ones who don't diet. It seems more out of politeness, really. A sense of politeness. As if it's rude to eat, to show hunger. I like a woman with a healthy appetite, who isn't afraid to eat; enjoys her food. Of course, you said that you had walked a lot today, isn't that right? And you got yourself lost and that's how you ended up here, on my doorstep. By accident. Walking." He pauses. "I mean, that would certainly explain your hunger. All that walking. All that exercise. Just the thing for building an appetite; sharpening the taste buds. People should actually walk more. It would do a world of good. Of course, it's difficult for some. More difficult for others. In fact, it's not a simple thing at all, for most folks. It's just too, too, I don't know — impossible? What I mean is, it starts out sounding like such a simple thing, when, in reality, it isn't so simple at all, is it? It's difficult. There are so many things, really, that are against it, that stand opposed to it that one, well, what I guess I'm saying is, you can plan it for years and years, right down to the last detail, and never step foot outside your door. Which isn't to say that isn't the best thing in the end, after all. Considering the objections and such. The difficulties. The risk involved. It probably is the best thing for all concerned. In the long run." She cleans up her plate, takes a deep breath, lays down her napkin and sighs. She smiles. "It's only my opinion, naturally. I don't claim to be an expert." She pushes away her plate and clears a piece of food inside her cheek with a crooked finger. "You were starving. When did you eat last?"

"This morning, I suppose."

"You suppose? You don't remember?"

She leans back in her chair and surveys the room. "You have a lovely place. Do you live here alone?"

"Yes. What about you? Where are you from?"

"But you were married at one time."

"Yes. Years ago. Where were you going when you landed here?"

"What happened to her?"

"Left me for someone else. A travelling salesman. Like in the jokes. Are you on holiday?"

"That's too bad. Children?"

"Dead. There were two of them, a boy and a girl. They drowned in a boating accident. Though at the time there was some talk of foul play. Suspicion fell on their mother, my wife. She wasn't well at the time. There were some problems." He laughs a small laugh. "Stupid, right? To believe that a mother could drown her own children?"

"I remember seeing a child once — a boy or a girl, it doesn't matter — wearing a t-shirt that read: If you love something set it free. If it comes back, it is yours to keep. If it doesn't come back, hunt it down and kill it."

"What is that supposed to mean?"

She hesitates. "Nothing. It's just something I saw."

"Who are you?"

Her voice and manner brighten. "Dinner was delicious. Did your mother teach you how to cook?"

"Necessity taught me. Why won't you answer any of my questions?"

"What?"

"You expect me to tell you everything about myself and refuse to tell me anything about you. Why?"

"It's unimportant."

"To who?"

"To me. Unimportant and uninteresting. It bores me

to talk about myself."

"I see. Well, will you tell me your name at least, so I know what to call you?"

"Miriam."

"Miriam? Are you sure?"

She regards him squarely. "What an odd question."

"I mean are you sure your name is Miriam and not Judith or Kathleen?"

"Whatever. If Miriam doesn't suit you, pick another. Am I sure? What is there to be sure of? Especially with something so common as a name."

"Don't be angry."

"I'm not."

"No. You're not. I can see that. You never get angry. And if I asked you to leave now, you would, wouldn't you? Without a fuss? Without question?"

"Yes."

"And if I asked you to stay, to spend the night here with me, in my bed, to make love with me, you'd also agree?"

"Yes."

"Why?"

"Because you want me to."

"That's all?"

"Isn't that enough?"

"Is it true — you remember nothing?" She takes her wine and sips it. He speaks quietly, as if to himself, yet loud enough for her to hear. "Not the smallest sign of recollection. Not caring, not even curious. It seems impossible. Who are you? What are you? A ghost? A witch? Some crazy escaped from the funny farm?"

"Shall I leave?"

"No. No, I want you to stay. This time — you do understand — this time, I want you to stay." She remains attentive, seemingly unmoved. "Do you have any idea what I'm talking about?" No reply. "Do you recognize me? Do you remember ever being here before?" Her tongue and lips make slight smacking sounds as she drinks. "You don't even try. You don't even make an effort. Doesn't it matter to you what happened three years ago or fourteen months ago? Doesn't it bother you that you can't remember when you last ate; where you were?"

"No. What matters is that I'm here now; that I'm full now."

"And tomorrow?"

"Tomorrow is a long way off. Whatever is going to happen will happen."

"And what has happened?"

"What has happened is past. Nothing to be done for it."

"No looking forward and no looking back and a bed for the night." His tone is harsh, though cautious.

"It suits me."

"It should frighten you. How do you know you won't be beaten or killed? Won't be raped some night or catch some sort of disease?"

"I don't. How do you know?" He sags into his chair. His mouth hangs open, moving, attempting to form words without the benefit of sound. He wipes his face with his hand and pulls at his jaw, massaging the faulty mechanism, coaxing the breath from his locked chest. Words tremble from his lips.

"Three years ago you showed up in pretty much the same way as you did this time; wearing a packsack, your hair wind-blown, tired, hungry, a bit dirty. You called yourself Kathleen. Told me your car had broken down somewhere on the road; that you'd lost your way searching for a shortcut. We didn't talk much. It didn't seem necessary. I fed you dinner. We drank apricot wine, put on a fire. We slept together. It seemed right, natural. The next morning we had planned to drive into town, to a gas station, then find your car. I wasn't convinced of the broken-down car story in the first place, but it was a plan of action, a way to be with you. When I woke up, you were already gone. I went into town anyway, made a few inquiries. No one could help. You had vanished. I let it drop. At least, I thought I let it drop. But I couldn't. I couldn't forget you. I started imagining the sound of your knock at the door. As though your knock was recognizable from the rest." He chuckles. "The number of bruises I've received running to answer your knock...anyway, some nights more than others I'd feel that you would return, and so I'd turn on the porch light. There'd be signs, you know: the sound of a bird, the discovery of a lost object, the arrangement of the sheets on the bed, the smell of apricots. Or maybe nothing so tangible. A memory that drops so quickly through the mind that it's just the memory of a memory: unrecognizable, yet enough to cause a quiver up the back, in the stomach. At some point I gave up on premonitions and left the light on every night, hoping, I suppose, that I could draw you to me, like a moth. Fourteen months ago, you were back." Without room for a break, she picks up the thread of the story and continues.

"It was July. The evening simmered with a dryness you could taste, brittle and tawny as straw. I walked to your door, it was still so bright it was impossible to tell if the light was on. I knocked. When you answered, I asked for a glass of water. You seemed surprised. I wondered if I was interrupting something or if my appearance was somehow displeasing. I pushed my hair back with my hand and shook my head. Dust filled the air, I couldn't breathe, I faltered. Whether from dust or fatigue or both, I was off-balance. You took my arm and led me inside. I drank some water, slowly. The slowest glass of water I had ever drunk. You invited me to stay for dinner. We drank apricot wine cold from the fridge. The heat was stifling. Still I asked you to put on the fireplace, and you set a few sticks burning. I suggested we remove our clothes and wash each other with damp towels, watching the flames glow orange across our wet bodies. We spent the night on the floor, drinking wine, making love and washing each other with soft, coloured towels and buckets of cool water." She takes a long draft of her wine, finishing the glass. He pours more from the bottle. "Is that the way it went?"

"Something like that. At any rate, the next morning, once again you were gone." She dampens the rim of her glass with her finger and causes it to sing.

"I was hoping it would be different this time. That you had come to stay."

"Stay? You mean forever?" She silences the glass, removing her finger and licking the tip. "That's impossible."

"Why? Are you afraid that after three days you'll turn into a pumpkin or something, like in the fairy tales?"

"Is that so unbelievable?"

"Can I ask you a question?"

"Isn't that what you've been doing?"

"You think I ask too many questions?"

"I think you expect too many answers."

"Look at me."

"I am."

"I mean, look at me closely; deeply. Look at me and tell me: who am I?"

"You mean you don't know?"

"I thought I did. But that was years ago; hundreds, thousands of years ago. Now, I'm not sure." He sighs and rubs his eyes with his palms. "When I was younger, in high school, you know, sixteen or seventeen, my friends — the guys — would play a sort of game. It was a sexual game, of course, and there was a point system involved that depended on how far you got with a girl. I can't remember all the details but it was very elaborate: say, a point for holding hands, two for a kiss, three for necking, four for rubbing her breast — and it had to be real rubbing, not a kind of accidental brush — five gets the bra off, six or eight diddles her...you get the idea — right up to ten where you actually..." He makes quote signs in the air with his fingers, "... fucked her. It was all based on the honour system," he laughs. "A rather strange use of the word, considering the circumstances, I suppose. Nevertheless, we'd get together after anyone had had a date or an encounter and hear the story and figure out the points. But there were also ways to lose points. This, of course, kept the game competitive, which was a problem for me. I liked being with the guys, being part of the group and listening to the stories, but I found it difficult to participate in the game. Except, to be a part of the gang meant having to be part of the game. You see, points were taken off if you went so many days without making an attempt to score." He finishes his wine and pours another glass.

"I mean, not all of the guys were what you'd call movers, but I was the only one who lost so many points that I was forever in the negatives. I was starting to get a reputation that maybe I was queer or something." He chews the corner of his fingernail, concentrating his eyes on his knuckles.

"Anyway, there was this one girl — I mean, if you were in need of a few easy points by the end of the week — there was this one girl who'd go all the way after a few shots of lemon gin. She knew the game. It didn't matter to her. Who knows, maybe the girls played the same game. Or their own variation. It doesn't matter. The guys were egging me on; joking. They threatened to kick me out of the group. Called me a fag, a homo. You know how cruel kids can be. So I asked her out, bought a bottle of gin from the local bootlegger, borrowed the old man's car and took her to some secluded back road. I didn't want to be surprised by the arrival of my pals checking up on me. We parked and started drinking right out of the bottle. We didn't talk. I stared at her rather stupidly. I wanted to get it over with and I didn't even know how to start. So I just stared at her. She wasn't pretty, kind of gawky and angular, all edges, but she wasn't ugly either. Everyone called her 'carrot top' or 'freckles'. Even the girls." He pauses, shakes his head as if to clear it.

"Anyhow, we drank some more gin, until we both had a nice glow on and things felt kind of dreamy. Then she lifted her ass off the seat and hiked up her skirt. She wasn't wearing underwear and I figured this is it, she'll just say: 'OK, big boy (or some other cliché), stick it in, get your rocks off, score your points and take me home.' Simple." He grabs the wine glass in both hands and brings it to his nose. He sniffs the bouquet. His eyes take in the woman.

"Except it wasn't like that. She grinned and pointed between her legs saying: 'If you want this, you'll have to do something for me first.' " He places the glass to his lips and drinks. "She wanted to make love. I mean, really make love. She guided me through and it was beautiful, not like the stories I'd heard at all; gentle, caring. And frightening. When it was over, I didn't know what to do or what to say. I wondered whether she had been like this with all the other guys or only with me, but I was afraid to ask. Meanwhile, she got dressed as though nothing had happened. She picked up the condom I had brought for the occasion off the floor and tucked it — still in its plastic wrapper — in my shirt pocket. Suddenly, I hated her. I hated her, because, while it was over for her, for me it had just begun. I wanted to lash out at her; hit her, smash her face in, call her names: slut, pig, whore. To free myself, you understand? To escape. Instead, I did nothing. I kept it inside. All the way back to her place we never spoke. I raced off, finished the gin and tried to throw up on the side of the road. I couldn't. I couldn't even get sick." There is a long silence in which the two do not move; their eyes meet. "How do you manage it?"

"What?"

"Living."

"I just…live."

"No secret, no magic formula?"

"I forget myself. I feel I am what happens in the room I'm in — not something else."

"Hmm. Sounds simple enough. But then, the impossible always does."

She gets up out of her chair and walks behind him. "What colour is the wall in front of you?"

"White."

She covers his eyes with her hands. "What colour now?"

"Still white?"

"Wrong. It's cream. Describe what's on the wall."

"It's bare?"

"Wrong. There's a picture. A seascape. Now do you see it?"

"Yes?"

"There's a boat. What colour is it?"

"Brown?"

"Wrong. It's green. How many fishermen in the boat?"

"Two?"

"Wrong. Three. What are their names?"

"This is ridiculous. How can I know the names of three people in a picture? In a picture that doesn't even exist?"

"A minute ago you agreed it did exist."

"What if I did? Anyway, it doesn't matter which three names I give you, you'll only tell me I'm wrong, right?"

"Poor boy. You turn every statement into a question. Names are less important than your ability to convince." He tears her hands from his face and spins around in his chair, holding her tight, his head pressed against the side of her hip.

"Now you describe for me the wall behind you."

"There is no wall. There is a field of marigolds that stretches to the horizon. An ocean of dazzling orange that robs the sun and coats the sky in a pane of blue ice. The only clouds crawl ponderous as dinosaurs within that frozen cube, their eyes clenched against the frost. Meanwhile, beneath their feet, a million miles away, the field undulates, weighed down by its own hot breath like some sleepy dragon. Bees make their floating buzz from flower to flower, as does the occasional hummingbird. Between the steaming land and the crystal sky a breeze perfumes the scene and the odour is not of one thing or another. It is less a sensation of smell than one of touch. One feels it — thick and humid — a pungency that clings to the skin and crawls through the pores. The internal organs melt, the bones melt, the flesh melts, the skin burns to fine golden ash that scatters and loses itself among the marigold petals. "He has released her hands and is sobbing, his tears flowing freely, staining her jeans. She cups his head, stroking his hair. He wraps his arms around her legs, buries his face in her belly, gently kisses the soft 'V' formed above her legs: the pubic area, hip bones and navel; his hands caressing her thighs, massaging her buttocks, the small of her back; allowing himself to be raised, by the slight pressure of her fingers, out of his chair, kissing in turn her breasts, neck, cheeks, ears, eyes, nose and finally, her mouth.

૨૦

She wakes to the sound of a nail being pounded into the outside of the window frame. She gets out of bed and goes to the door. She tries the handle, it turns, but the door is bolted shut. She lingers a moment, fingers the lock, leans her face against the wood, then returns to bed. She sits, regards her naked body, runs a hand along her amber skin, holds an arm up to the light and squints. She collapses back onto the pillow and covers herself with the sheet. When the door bolt slides open, she doesn't budge. He enters with a tray, closes the door, and secures the bolt.

"Good morning. I've brought you breakfast. I understand your not wanting to talk to me; to look at me. I do. But you have to understand as well, from my point of view, it can't continue like this, with you coming and going. I can't bear it…a few hours of happiness compared with months and years of sadness. I want you here with me; always. You'll see, everything will turn out for the best. I have to have you. You have to stay. It isn't right, you see, what you're doing. It's no life."

He sets the tray down beside her on the end of the table and sits on the bed. He strokes her forehead. She doesn't respond.

"I'm right about this. You have to believe me. You have to understand. I'm going crazy. I can't live without you. Since you left I've dreamed the same dream night after night. Shall I tell you?" She closes her eyes; a small tear presses from beneath the lids.

"I'm searching for you. Looking everywhere, asking everyone I meet. No one knows anything about you. No one's seen you. Scenes race by like a movie going in fast-forward. I only catch glimpses. Places I've never been to, faces I've never seen. At least, nothing I can remember. Suddenly, I'm being led down a hallway. I can only see the back of the person leading me — a woman in some type of nurse's uniform. Her hand waves me past numerous heavy, locked doors. Finally, we stop and enter one of the cells. In the corner is a woman all bunched up in a grey gown, her face against the wall, covered by her arms — her bare arms pale, except for a pattern of garish specks." He wipes a tear from his cheek. "That's all I can make out: her arms and, of course, her hair." He wraps a lock of her hair around a finger. "Hair much like yours, tangled and rusty, like a mass of copper wire left too long in the elements. The nurse taps the woman's shoulder to get her attention and as she turns toward me…" He bites his lip. "As she turns to face me, I cover my eyes. I can't tear my hands away. I can't force myself to look at her. I'm too afraid…too afraid. Then the dream is over. I wake up."

"Are you afraid that the face you see will be mine?"

"No. I'm afraid it will be my own."

"I also have a dream. I dream that I am a shoe surrounded by a world of feet. The feet want to wear me, naturally. They try to slip into me, but none fit. I'm either too big or too small. Still, they keep at me, not knowing what else to do."

"Is that really your dream?"

"No. I made it up. I never dream."

"Your breakfast is getting cold. I'll leave you now." He walks to the door and unlocks the bolt. The door opens, behind him is a crash of glass and cutlery on the floor. She remains lying on the bed, her head rolled on the pillow, facing him as he slowly turns.

"Why do you hate me so?" Her voice is low, but clear. He steps out of the room and closes the door. The bolt slides shut.

ই

"I've brought you a bowl of apricots." He sets the bowl on the end table and cleans up the previous day's breakfast off the floor as he speaks. "I know how you love apricots. I remember the one time when there were fresh apricots on the table and you picked out one to eat — picked out, mind you, as though it was the best of the bunch. Almost as if, rather than you choosing it, it had chosen you. You didn't eat it right away. Instead, you held it in your palm, stroked its fur with your fingers as though it were a tiny animal. You raised it to the light, studying every smooth line, seemingly fascinated by its shape, entranced by its colour. Then you transported it to your mouth as a kind of offering. You closed your eyes, your lips parted — I could tell you were tasting it even before your teeth had penetrated the flesh, before your tongue had tasted the juice. And it wasn't just a pleasure of the mind, you were able to enjoy it with your entire body. It was hypnotic. Watching you, I couldn't help but think that the flavour of the actual apricot would be a disappointment. I was wrong. You bit into the fruit and it was like…like…I don't know. I can't describe it. I don't have the words. There are none. I wanted to cry. I guess that's what it was like." He takes an apricot from the bowl.

"I love the way you handle an object. The way you examine it. You have the marvellous ability to make the simplest things precious. I love watching you eat." He holds the apricot beneath her nose. She doesn't move. She refuses to even sniff at it.

"Please. You must eat something." He rubs her lips lightly with the fruit. "Please." He lays it on her pillow. A hand emerges from the sheet. She takes the apricot and slowly lifts it up to the light. He stands back to watch. She poses like this for a moment, then releases her grip. The apricot drops to the floor.

"Yesterday my skin was tanned. The light barely penetrated. Today it's like rice paper. I can see every vein. By tomorrow morning I'll be a puff of smoke and by evening a ghost smothered among the white sheets." Her arm snakes back beneath the covers. He drags himself out the door.

ҙ☙

He stands trembling in the doorway, eyeing her form, motionless except for a faint shiver of breath. A column of light breaks across her body, blurring the sharp edges of her skin and stoking her wild hair to flames. He pushes the door, the handle bangs against the wall. He turns, walks to the living room and sits in a chair facing away from the front door. He picks up a cloth and a rifle and polishes the barrel. Sounds filter from the bedroom: the creak of bedsprings, the shuffle of feet, the slap and zip of clothing being put on, the march of boots moving without hesitation out of the bedroom, through the living room, down the hallway, then the opening of the door and the final click. He carries the rifle into the bedroom and crosses to the bed. He sits on the edge, the butt of the rifle set between his legs. On the pillow lie three apricots, split in half, their stones removed. He reaches out a hand and traces a finger around the moist edge of each apricot section. He licks the tip of his finger. The rifle slips from his grip and falls to the floor. He crawls into bed, rests his head on the pillow, closes his eyes, and slowly, indulgently, devours each apricot, one by one.

notes

SKIN DEEP

Since the text derives in large part from an article in the *National Enquirer* (October 1990), the characters should be assumed to be completely fictional and no comparison should be made between any persons living or dead (or living and dead).

As well, there should be no attempt to construe the story as a re-telling of the "Frankenstein" myth from a male perspective. My ambitions have never been so lofty.

The phrase "bathed in a slice of moonlight" has obvious apocrypha connotations, so the less said, the better.

Finally, apologies to my mother-in-law who read the story in magazine form and hasn't looked at me or my work in the same way since.

LATE-NIGHT SUBWAY

Pierre Moule (1932-1961), French poet, rode the Paris metro constantly as a source of inspiration. His most famous poem, "Woman In The Window" (1955), derived in part from the story "Woman At The Window" (1897) by Otto Leip (1872-1924), and, as well, suggested "Woman Outside The Window" (1985), a New Age/neo-feminist/Jungian tract (this description taken from the book jacket) written by the noted American philologist/amateur aviatrix and professor poeticus et historiarum at the University of California, Hosanna Gladioli (1948-).

The poem "Pass Void" (1972) by Henri Moule (1949-1978) — no relation to Pierre — accounts for Pierre's mysterious disappearance one night inside the dank tunnels and also served to establish the "myth" of Pierre Moule (aka: *Peter the Mole*, so familiar to everyone by now via the underground comic trade that I won't bore you with the details any further).

HOME, AFTER ALL

I can only answer the critic's sharp attacks with a gentle rebuff: "If you steal from one author, it's plagiarism; if you steal from many, it's research." (Wilson Mizner [1876-1933], quoted in John Burke's *Rogue's Progress*).

THE ANT GAME

Section 1 contains a variant of a sentence by the West Coast poet Woody Haze (1926-): "The grass always needs mowing."

Section 4 is a joke told to me by a twelve-year-old child, though I know that I recall the joke from my own childhood. At any rate, a bad joke that, nevertheless, persists.

Section 5 contains variants of two sentences by the Prairie writer Ernestine d'Angelo (1868-1967): "The snows were e'er upon her hair," from the poem "Mother" and "My Life, my yarn, my barn," from the poem "My Life, My Yarn, My Barn."

The ant game is a children's game wherein one person chooses someone from a crowd and follows them for as long as possible without losing them.

I DON'T HAVE A PROBLEM
"All connected with the film agree that White [Vanna] doffed her clothes reluctantly and refused to go topless in her dance scene." (*People Weekly*, June 6, 1988).

ONCE UPON A TIME
Follows two dictums of Blaise Pascal (1623-1662): (i) "Things are always at their best in their beginning" and (ii) "One only knows how to begin when one reaches the end."

NOTES
Thanks to Hans Joachim Schadlich (1935-) and his fine book of short stories, *Approximation*.

Bootlegging Apples on the Road to Redemption
by Mary Elizabeth Grace

This is Grace's first collection of poetry. It is an exploration of the collective self, about all of us trying to find peace; this is a collection of poetry about searching for the truth of one's story and how it is never heard or told, it is only experienced. It is the second story, our attempts with words to express the sounds and images of the soul. Her writing is soulful, intricate and lyrical. The book comes with a companion CD of music/poetry compositions which are included in the book.

5 1/4" x 8 1/4" • 80 pages • trade paperback with cd • isbn 1-895837-30-8 • $21.99

The Last Word: an insomniac anthology of canadian poetry
edited by michael holmes

The Last Word is a snapshot of the next generation of Canadian poets, the poets who will be taught in schools — voices reflecting the '90s and a new type of writing sensibility. The anthology brings together 51 poets from across Canada, reaching into different regional, ethnic, sexual and social groups. This varied and volatile collection pushes the notion of an anthology to its limits, like a startling Polaroid. Proceeds from the sale of *The Last Word* will go to Frontier College, in support of literacy programs across Canada.

5 1/4" x 8 1/4" • 168 pages • trade paperback • isbn 1-895837-32-4 • $16.99

Desire High Heels Red Wine
Timothy Archer, Sky Gilbert, Sonja Mills and Margaret Webb

Sweet, seductive, dark and illegal; this is *Desire, High Heels, Red Wine*, a collection by four gay and lesbian writers. The writing ranges from the abrasive comedy of Sonja Mills to the lyrical and insightful poetry of Margaret Webb, from the campy dialogue of Sky Gilbert to the finely crafted short stories of Timothy Archer. Their writings depict dark, abrasive places populated by bitch divas, leather-clad bodies, and an intuitive sense of sexuality and gender. The writers' works are brought together in an elaborate and striking design by three young designers.

5 1/4" x 8 1/4" • 96 pages • trade paperback • isbn 1-895837-26-X • $12.99

Beds & Shotguns

Diana Fitzgerald Bryden, Paul Howell McCafferty, Tricia Postle and Death Waits

Beds & Shotguns is a metaphor for the extremes of love. It is also a collection by four emerging poets who write about the gamut of experiences between these opposites from romantic to obsessive, fantastic to possessive. These poems and stories capture love in its broadest meanings and are set against a dynamic, lyrical landscape.

5 1/4" x 8 1/4" • 96 pages • trade paperback • isbn 1-895837-28-6 • $13.99

Playing in the Asphalt Garden

Phlip Arima, Jill Battson, Tatiana Freire-Lizama and Stan Rogal

This book features new Canadian urban writers, who express the urban experience — not the city of buildings and streets, but as a concentration of human experience, where a rapid and voluminous exchange of ideas, messages, power and beliefs takes place.

5 3/4" x 9" • 128 pages • trade paperback • isbn 1-895837-20-0 • $14.99

Mad Angels and Amphetamines

Nik Beat, Mary Elizabeth Grace, Noah Leznoff and Matthew Remski

A collection by four emerging Canadian writers and three graphic designers. In this book, design is an integral part of the prose and poetry. Each writer collaborated with a designer so that the graphic design is an interpretation of the writer's works. Nik Beat's lyrical and unpretentious poetry; Noah Leznoff's darkly humourous prose and narrative poetic cycles; Mary Elizabeth Grace's Celtic dialogues and mystical images; and Matthew Remski's medieval symbols and surrealistic style of story; this is the mixture of styles that weave together in *Mad Angels and Amphetamines*.

6" x 9" • 96 pages • trade paperback • isbn 1-895837-14-6 • $12.95

Insomniac Press • 378 Delaware Ave. • Toronto, ON, Canada • M6H 2T8
phone: (416) 536-4308 • fax: (416) 588-4198